It's Our Planet Too

DO BIRDS YEARN FOR FREEDOM JUST AS WE DO?

PRIYA PAUL

BLUEROSE PUBLISHERS
India | U.K.

Copyright © Priya Paul 2023

All rights reserved by author. No part of this publication may be reproduced, stored in a retrieval system or transmitted in any form or by any means, electronic, mechanical, photocopying, recording or otherwise, without the prior permission of the author. Although every precaution has been taken to verify the accuracy of the information contained herein, the publisher assumes no responsibility for any errors or omissions. No liability is assumed for damages that may result from the use of information contained within.

BlueRose Publishers takes no responsibility for any damages, losses, or liabilities that may arise from the use or misuse of the information, products, or services provided in this publication.

For permissions requests or inquiries regarding this publication, please contact:

BLUEROSE PUBLISHERS
www.BlueRoseONE.com
info@bluerosepublishers.com
+91 8882 898 898
+4407342408967

ISBN: 978-93-5819-816-4

Cover Design: Muskan Sachdeva
Typesetting: Pooja Sharma

First Edition: December 2023

What People Have To Say

We need to recognize Parrots and birds as sentient beings that require as many natural elements and freedoms as we humans need to live happy lives

Christopher Castle.
Macaw Conservation

Your book is a great initiative that will help create awareness about the rights of animals and will go a long way in informing people that birds belong in the wild and not in cages.

Peta India

I am happy you have written a book on foreign birds in India.

Maneka Sanjay Gandhi
People for Animals

People are too used to seeing them as pets and have forgotten how needed they are in the wild. That's why books like this are so important.

Carey Witlz
Macaw Recovery Network

Acknowledgement

It's such a pleasure to write this Thanksgiving note and I would thus like to begin with my daughter, Myra, for helping me throughout my book. From the conceptualisation of the story to the climax, you stood tall beside me, hearing all the craziness since the beginning. I am grateful for your critical input and patience even when I read out the same chapters twice to you. Thank you, darling, for being with me throughout the course of this book.

Shanaya, my little one, you giggled and laughed at all the crazy anecdotes mentioned in the book and that encouraged me greatly.

Rajat, thank you for constantly pushing me to complete this book when I dealt with writer's block or felt tired.

Special thanks to Christopher Castle, Janice Jobson and my other mates for sharing your first-hand experiences and insightful stories pertaining to the rescue and rehabilitation of birds.

Thank you, Kush, Krish, Prayan – this book is for you, kiddos.

Lastly, thank you, Frosty for giving me company till late at night by just being beside me without making any noise.

Contents

1. Kavya 1
2. Captain 6
3. En Route to Kochipuram 9
4. Kavya and Grandpa 16
5. Best Buddies 19
6. Satya 23
7. Evil Spirit 27
8. The Mulberry Tree 33
9. Bitter and Sweet Experiences 38
10. Back To School 39
11. Field Trip 42
12. Trip to Spandhan 45
13. Sunday Funday 58
14. Kavya and the Macaw 64
15. Mt Halton School 65
16. Kavya and the Principal 70
17. Unfulfilled Dreams 73
18. Sudha 77
19. Crazy Bunch 87
20. Changemaker 95
21. Presentation Day 99

22. Jonah 101

23. Silver Lining 106

24. Maiden Flight to Honduras 108

25. Welcome to Honduras 111

26. Macaw Mountain 114

1. Kavya

During the hot summer month of June, a little girl called Kavya was peddling her bicycle home as fast as she could. The scorching sun was blazing down, making the roads of Trivandrum – a scenic town in the coastal belt of the western ghats – a baker's oven radiating heat.

Despite the uncomfortable weather, little Kavya, who was undeterred by the angry sun, was peddling furiously. Every peddle followed the other in a cyclical motion, her cheeks were turning red and rivulets of sweat were streaming down her forehead, her hair was neatly parted into two plaits, and tied with red ribbons at the bottom making two perfect bows.

She raced into the compound and pushed open the iron gate of her house with one hand while she wheeled her cycle in with the other.

'Maa! Maa! Maa!' her voice was shrill and demanding, and with each successive 'Maa', growing louder than the doorbell.

That's what Mrs Murthy always said about her daughter, 'She doesn't need a doorbell!'

Kavya hugged her mother. 'Maa, exam over! Now listen, I will sleep late, I will wake up late and I won't take a bath on Sunday! Oh, and one more thing, I'm not going to touch my books now!'

'Kavya, just stop! Look at yourself. You look like a dust magnet picking up whatever dirt comes your way. Go and take a bath immediately,' said her mum.

'Ok, ok. Maa, what's for lunch? I am so hungry,' said Kavya.

With a pleased smile, Mrs Murthy said, 'Rasam rice.'

'Oh, Maa, we had rasam rice the day before yesterday,' Kavya grumbled.

'That was sambar rice, Kavya,' her mother placated her, going on to explain the differences between the two most popular dishes of South India.

'But Maa-'

'Go now, Kavya and take a bath quickly. I am also very hungry and have not eaten a single morsel since this morning.'

Mrs Murthy, Kavya's mother, was a religious lady born and brought up in a typical Brahmin family. According to her, there was only one thing that could bring peace to the human race – religion. She was a religious lady who embodied discipline as one of the daily chores of life.

With the first rays of the sun heralding a new day, one could find Mrs Murthy draped in a freshly, starched, crisp, cotton saree, her long hair entwined with a towel forming a knot at the nape of her neck, her broad forehead marked with red vermilion in a small round *bindi*. (A bindi is also believed to be the third eye as per Hinduism and is worn to ward off bad luck).

Kavya came out of the bathroom after an hour, wearing a light blue frock, her shoulder-length hair now curled up to her neck.

'Oh, what were you doing in there for so long?' enquired Mrs Murthy. 'And what is this? Can't you wipe the floor after using the bathroom? And who will switch off the light?'

'Hungry, Maa...Food!' shrieked Kavya.

She sat at the dining table with a bowl filled with soupy rasam and white rice, a few mustard seeds and curry leaves floating on top of the rasam. Kavya filled her spoon with the piping hot rasam and slurped it down.

'Mmmm, yummy!'

Her mother smiled at her with a sense of satisfaction and served herself some rasam and rice and started mixing the two with her long slender fingers. 'Nice, na?' She gulped down her small rasam-rice balls one by one.

'Achha, listen, we are going to Kochipuram to your grandpa's house tomorrow.'

'Really, Maa? You are my darling!' Kavya jumped up and kissed her mother with a mouth full of food. 'Oh, I am so happy!'

'Oh, oh, Kavya! What are you doing? Finish your food first,' said her mother, pretending to be angry.

'Your father is checking the availability of bus tickets – but most probably we'll be going tomorrow morning, so we need to pack our stuff.'

'Maa, you have made me so happy.' She then dropped her spoon and used her fingers to relish the magic of eating rice in a typical South Indian style. A few more slurps later, her bowl was licked clean.

'Maa, my clothes?' enquired Kavya.

'I have done your packing', said Mrs Murthy in a reassuring voice. 'You just have to look over it once in case you want to pack something else.'

'Hey, Maa, what about Grandpa's mango pickle and his favourite *black lentil papadum?*'

Mrs Murthy smiled while pulling Kavya's cheek. 'All done, baby. *Achar* for your grandpa and *papadum* is already packed, I just have to collect his kurta from the market, and all my work is done.'

'Hmm, impressed,' said Kavya with a cheeky smile.

'Now you go and get some rest,' said Mrs Murthy.

Kavya turned around with her smile intact and excitement in her eyes and moved toward her room. She lay down on her bed tugging the pillow between her legs and closed her eyes. She could see her maternal grandparent's house just like a picture – a huge single-storey bungalow with a rustic brown exterior and a thatched roof.

An open and wide verandah running all around the house. She reminisced about her past vacations spent at her grandpa's house; a giant mulberry tree in the middle of the yard, giving food year-round to the hundreds of birds that came visiting for a sweet treat.

She pictured herself playing hide-n-seek, hiding behind the stack of jute sacks full of rice, while Satya chased her, and then, she opened her eyes. Satya was her best friend. Her excitement doubled at the thought of meeting him.

Satya was the son of Mr Ravikant who owned the majority of farmland in that region and happened to be a good friend of Grandpa. And as luck would have it, he was also their next-door neighbour.

Kavya tossed and turned as she couldn't sleep with excitement; she got up from her wooden bed which made a creaking sound with every move she made and went to check on the stuff that was already packed.

Something is missing, she thought with a mischievous smile and rushed towards her cupboard, opened it and started taking out a few things. Her sketchbook, a mouth organ, and then she picked up her gold medallion hanging next to her study table. She wanted to show off all these possessions to her grandpa, whom she referred to as Dadu.

Once her checklist was done, she sat down peacefully with a hairbrush in her hand, trying to take out the knots from her unimaginably tangled hair. It reached her waist when she pulled it straight but would spring back again to rest on her shoulders. She wondered if it would ever grow long and straight. In between this complicated scenario, she suddenly remembered that she needed to say goodbye to someone.

Someone very precious to Kavya – her very special friend – Captain.

2. Captain

'Hey, Surya,' said Kavya in her chirpy voice, raising herself on her toes and resting her hand and her chin on the boundary wall of their garden which served as a partition between each bungalow. All the houses were built in a row with almost the same external façade.

Surya was the son of Mr and Mrs Iyer, their next-door neighbour, and they had relocated from America a couple of years ago. Surya enjoyed chatting about how big and revolutionised things were in the US. He loved taking centre-stage among the kids of the neighbourhood and talking about how much improvement was needed here, comparing the differences in the way of life between the two countries.

'You know what, the schools in America are much friendlier, and the teachers…they don't give homework,' Surya would say and have all the kids listen to him with rapt attention with their mouths agape.

'And you know what the biggest difference is? Teachers don't beat students!'

'Even if they misbehave?' asked one kid in utter surprise.

'No, of course not.'

But Kavya was not at all impressed by his airs; the only thing that kept her coming back to him was his pet parrot, Captain, of whom she was very fond.

'Hey, Surya,' said Kavya, greeting him.

'Hi! What's up, Kavya?' responded Surya.

'How is Captain? Can I meet him?'

'Hmm, I don't know, he is there in the backyard, go check it out yourself.' And then he continued regaling everyone with his tales.

Kavya smiled and ran to the back of the bungalow. Before she could say anything, loud squawking sounds started coming from the end.

'Welcome, Kavya! Welcome, Kavya!' And it kept getting louder and louder.

'Hello, Captain, how are you?'

She gently stroked his feathers with her finger and Captain started responding to her affectionate gesture.

She pulled out some bird feed from her pocket and fed him with great affection. However busy little Kavya was, she always ensured to come and play with Captain for at least 15 -20 minutes.

'You know, Captain, I am going to my grandpa's house for ten days, so please don't become grumpy when I'm away. I will be back soon with new, fresh crispy corn seeds for you. Now, I have to go.'

'I will miss you, Captain,' she said, gently swinging his cage from side to side. 'But I will come back soon. Don't get grumpy now, okay?'

Kavya said goodbye to her beloved parrot with a heavy heart. The parrot didn't belong to her, but the little bird had developed a bond with Kavya, and for that, even if she had to put up with Surya's tantrums, she was okay.

'Bye, Captain.'

'Bye, Kavya! Bye, Kavya! Bye, Kavya!' squawked the little bird till he saw his friend disappear from sight.

Surya disliked Kavya but didn't want to say anything as he liked to be in everybody's good books. He was, after all, a very image-conscious boy.

Once Kavya left, Surya went to the backyard and kept walking closer and closer to Captain's cage, but Captain didn't greet him. *I think he hasn't seen me.*

'Hello, Captain.' Captain didn't say anything. 'Hello, Captain!' he said again but this time in a louder voice.

But Captain didn't budge, rather he pretended to be asleep.

'Oh, this sleepy, useless bird, you are so lazy,' said Surya to himself and pushed the cage so forcefully that it left the parrot swinging to and fro and had him shrieking in anger.

3. En Route to Kochipuram

'Life is a journey. When we stop, things don't go right.' One must savour the journey, as it tends to be more beautiful than the destination. With every passing kilometre, the demographics of the locals kept changing. A few passengers would board the bus, while a few would get off, and others would get ready to get off at their stop coming soon.

Different faces - different stories; some looked so keen on initiating a chitchat with a co-passenger, while others kept their mouths sealed tight throughout the ride.

Once Kavya boarded the bus, her primary desire was to get a window seat. Travelling without a window seat was like a journey wasted – and she managed to get one by requesting the conductor. Sometimes by pretending to be nauseous, one could get a window seat – the most coveted one for the ride.

Observing and forming an opinion about people was Kavya's favourite pastime. She knew that all the passengers who were either sitting or standing, hanging onto the overhead bar by a single loop, had a story to tell, but the one who caught her attention was a man who had just boarded the bus with two wicker baskets. The basket had tiny gaps in it and as she watched carefully, she noticed something really interesting and amusing. Colourful feathers were peeking out from the gaps here and there.

'Are these birds? Oh, it's a real one...Oh, so many, look, Maa!' said Kavya.

'Don't point your finger,' said Mrs Murthy

'Maa, I can see so many birds in there.'

'Hmm, they do look like birds,' agreed Mrs Murthy.

'Oh, wow, he is lucky to have so many birds.'

It started raining after a while and Kavya was enjoying the gentle shower on her face. However, the lady sitting behind her found the same quite unpleasant and complained to Kavya to shut down the window. In buses of South India, one big window was shared by two passengers, and therefore, Kavya was forced to roll down the glass window. She was furious with the lady who was sitting right behind her and surprised that she didn't want even a single drop of water to come in.

Nonetheless, Kavya looked out at every passing tree, admiring Mother Nature in all her glory. Mrs Murthy tried to relish a few moments of peace, by trying to catch a quick power nap. She settled down into a comfortable position in her seat and placed a small pillow against her neck.

Kavya nudged her with her elbow.

Mrs Murthy tilted her face and opened one tired eye. 'What Kavya?'

'My tummy is asking for something, I'm a little hungry.'

Her mother shook her head in exasperation and bent forward to slowly lift the bag which was placed below the seat of the passenger sitting in front of her.

'Biscuits?'

'No Maa'

'Then?' enquired Mrs Murthy, in an annoyed tone.

'Hmm, sweet tamarind.'

Mrs Murthy took out a packet of tamarind which was packed with a sticky seal, assuring the pack remain fresh and untouched. Using her sharp nail, she made a small puncture in the outer packaging and then slowly peeled the cover off.

Chomp, chomp, chomp... Kavya was enjoying her tamarind and chewing at it noisily. Mrs Murthy opened one eye and glared at Kavya.

'Oh, sorry,' apologised Kavya and started quietly licking and sucking the tamarind, ensuring that there were no further loud eating noises from her as she collected all the tamarind seeds carefully in her pocket.

The bus stopped at Trichipura, which was about an hour and thirty minutes from Kochipuram. Here the bus stopped for 20 minutes. The conductor announced a tea-and-snack break and people got down for refreshments and to stretch their legs.

Kavya was sitting all relaxed in her seat, gazing at the drizzling rain and enjoying her sweet and sour tamarind.

Almost all the passengers had got down, some for coffee and some for snacks.

Eventually, she saw the tall old man who had been carrying the bird basket get off the bus. And through those tiny holes, Kavya could only see a cage stuffed with colourful feathers.

Are they real birds? she wondered.

The man was wearing a kurta and a dhoti, his ears were pierced, and he sported some big metal rectangular studs.

Instead of going towards the *dhaba*, the old man walked over to the other side of the highway. He sat there on the pavement divider and opened his basket.

There were real birds inside! Kavya couldn't contain her excitement.

He flipped the birds over one by one and took five of them out of the basket. They were either sleepy or dead, and he threw them out to one side. Then he took out two birds and held them upside down with their claws. They spread their red and green wings and flapped about as fast as they could, but couldn't move an inch.

He put them back into the basket, took out something from his pocket that looked like bird feed, and sprinkled it in the cage.

He closed the lid and walked back in the direction of the bus towards the *dhaba*; went inside and asked for a cup of tea. The *dhaba* owner didn't charge him anything as he squatted down next to his belongings and sipped the tea with a blissful expression.

Kavya couldn't believe what she had just seen.

How could he be so callous and unfeeling after losing so many pets?

She desperately wanted to get down and check on those dying or dead birds.

Fear and anger made her numb. She couldn't utter a word nor was she able to understand what was happening. She closed her eyes pretending to sleep, but her brain was just bombarding her with questions about what she had just seen. Gusts of wind coming from the window made it physically tiring for little Kavya to stay attentive and soon, she dozed off.

Mrs Murthy settled down next to Kavya and slowly, the bus moved on.

With a sudden jerk, a loud screeching sound and an irritating honk, the bus slowed down.

The conductor announced loudly, 'Kochipuram! Passengers be ready.'

'Kochipuram!' The word was like a sudden wake-up alarm for Mrs Murthy as it pulled her out of her dreamland. She always stayed attentive while travelling but somehow, she had fallen asleep this time.

She shook Kavya awake and pulled her upright with one hand and grabbed her luggage with the other.

'We are here, Kavya. Arey, what is this? Why did you take off your slippers?' asked Mrs Murthy, annoyed.

'Uhh, Maa...' Rubbing her eyes, Kavya stretched out her leg to find the other. 'Can't find it, Maa,' she announced in a worried tone.

Mrs Murthy bent down murmuring something in Malayalam.

'Sorry, Maa,' whispered Kavya.

'What sorry...' said Mrs Murthy, still very annoyed.

'What happened, madam?' asked the conductor in a loud voice.

'Arey, my daughter's slipper, can't find it!'

The conductor requested everyone to look under their seats.

'Here it is,' a voice announced jubilantly from two rows behind them. The middle-aged man went on to explain,

'Must have slid there with the insane way the driver hit the brake.'

'Thank you so much, uncle...'

Kavya, craned her neck out of the window, ducking low to squeeze her head through the window.

'Oh, Maa, look! Grandpa!' announced Kavya with excitement in her voice.

There stood Mr Gopal Das, a 6-foot-1-inch tall man with a dark complexion, wearing crispy, starched white kurta and dhoti. He signalled the bus to stop and the engine rumbled to a halt.

He instructed Ramu Anna to escort us off the bus. Ramu Anna had been working with Grandpa since his childhood, He was short and plump with a brilliant smile that was ever-ready to flash, and jet-black hair combed neatly and fixed in place with coconut oil.

Ramu Anna hurried in and took our luggage as he held my hand.

As this emotional reunion was going on, the bus started up again and moved ahead swiftly.

Grandpa's house was just five minutes from the bus stop. Grandpa called the *tangaa wala* and asked Kavya, 'So, little princess, would you like to travel on a royal chariot?'

Kavya giggled, hiding her face in Maa's saree, trying to hide her missing tooth.

It was spiritually reviving to breathe in the fresh air as everything around them was screaming life and positivity. The canal that surrounded the entire village was zigzagging around the area and cutting a path of its own; this lent a lyrical piece of background music to the panoramic view that looked as if a picture had come to life.

Grandpa was a very sociable person who loved to enquire about the well-being of their extended family, their neighbours, their children, their well-being, and their ailments.

Whatever the conversation or discussion was, it had to end with the advantages of living close to nature. The importance of pure milk, organic produce, and home-cooked food was the reason he stood strong, leading a sickness-free life.

4. Kavya and Grandpa

Sitting on the open verandah of the house, Kavya was spellbound at the sight of parrots that came into their ancestral home.

'Grandpa, they look so beautiful I just want to keep them with me,' said Kavya wistfully.

'Keep them? What do you mean, Kavya? You already have them. They come to your house, stay there, eat, and fly back. What else would you want?'

'No, Grandpa, not like that. I mean I want to keep them with me forever and ever.'

'Forever and ever, hmm,' repeated Mr Gopal Das.

'So, when I was your age, I too wanted to keep them with me forever and ever.'

'Then want happened, Grandpa?'

'I insisted that my parents get me a parrot, and guess what? I got one on my 10th birthday. We brought home a green parrot with a shiny red beak. I named him Sitaram.'

'Sitaram? That's too big a name for such a little creature. If I get a chance, I will name it Cashew.'

'Cashew…Wow, that's a nice name,' said Grandpa.

'Then what happened?' asked Kavya, listening with rapt attention.

'That day was the happiest day of my life as I found a friend and a companion in Sitaram. But for Sitaram, sadly, things were not the same. The little bird had lost all its friends and his beautiful world was taken away from him. I felt sad for Sitaram as he couldn't be the same chirpy, happy parrot as before, but had turned into a showpiece in my house.

'And one day, it died. I realised that Sitaram didn't die a natural death, but because of loneliness. He yearned for those free flights, the open skies, those companions. These beautiful birds never live alone, and if they get separated from their flock mates for even a moment, they call out wildly to them to be rescued.

'I cried a lot, and in the memory of my Sitaram, I started caring and feeding these birds. I care for them and arrange for their food and water. Now, look, my guava tree has a hundred Sitarams!'

Their ancestral home was like a mini bird sanctuary, where all little creatures were respected and allowed to enjoy themselves under the open sky. The entire village had followed the principle of not caging any birds and treated it as a bad omen if done so.

The uniqueness of the village was that they enjoyed a special bond with their feathered friends. In every household, one could find a bird feeder hanging either on a branch of a tree together with a pot of water, or on the rooftop of the house.

'Human beings have a basic disorder or perhaps a flaw in their emotional structure. The moment we love something, you know what happens?' asked Grandpa.

'**I want it!**' said Kavya in an excited tone.

'Yes, exactly, and that's the problem. The greed and desire to "possess", to take over.

Our foolishness and selfishness should not hamper the freedom and liberty of other living beings and turn them into mere objects. Birds are not meant to live in cages, they are born to fly. Flying is as natural to them as walking is to us. Stealing their freedom by capturing them and putting them into small cages is inhuman and cruel.

'Most importantly, Kavya, it is illegal.'

'What! Are you serious, Grandpa? Keeping a bird in a cage and feeding it is illegal?'

'Yes, it's illegal,' confirmed Grandpa.

'But Grandpa, parrots are kept in many households as a pet. Is it still illegal even if we take good care of it?'

'Yes, it is.'

'How is that possible, Grandpa? Parrots and love birds are seen in most houses and the police never say anything about them.'

Kavya went to sleep that night thinking about Sitaram and his fate. How sad he must've felt and the fact that Grandpa probably wasn't able to take good care of him. If she had been there, Sitaram would not have felt bad and fallen sick.

5. Best Buddies

Kavya was gobbling her breakfast when she asked her mother, 'Has Satya come to see us?'

'Who? Satya! I forgot to tell you, they have gone out on vacation.'

'Really, Maa? I will get bored here then. Why didn't you tell me this in the first place?' said Kavya with a frown on her face.

'I'm just joking. Finish your breakfast and go and check it out yourself what is keeping him so busy.'

'Maa, you are very bad,' pouted Kavya. 'I'm going now, bye.'

'Oh, finish this- Kavya!'

'Bye, Maa!'

She ran straight to Satya's house. It was a huge colonial bungalow with two entrance gates, however, one was usually kept locked according to the suggestion of their *vastu* consultant and only one gate was used by everyone. Upon entering, there was a well-laid-out garden with hybrid roses of big, beautiful blooms in a range of magnificent colours, but more often than not, these were not very perfumed or fragrant. Beyond the garden was a pebbled porch leading up to the main door.

She walked past the garden and went towards the lobby, an area connecting the kitchen garden and a partially covered kitchen.

She stepped in sneakily and covered Prabha Chachi's eyes from behind.

'Guess who?' asked Kavya in a cheeky voice.

Prabha affectionately touched Kavya's soft and podgy hands and said, 'Savita, hide all the mango pickles from the kitchen, our cute pickle thief is here!'

Savita and her family had been working in Satya's house as domestic help for the past two generations. Her husband worked as a driver for Mr Rameshwar.

'Oh, no, Chachi!' Kavya exclaimed, stomping her foot on the floor. 'How did you know it was me?'

'From your baby-soft hands. Now, leave this, how is your mother, tell me?' enquired Prabha.

'Chachi, she is fine, where is Satya?' muttered Kavya.

'He is upstairs, on the terrace. Listen, tell your mum that I will come to see her in the evening.'

'Okay, Chachi.'

Kavya ran upstairs and reached the terrace. Gathering her breath, she looked around and saw Satya sitting in a corner of the terrace, next to a bench, doing something crazy.

'Satya!' Kavya called out his name with delight.

'Kavya, when did you come? Come quickly, I want to show you something,' said Satya with a happy smile and lifted the top off a wicker basket.

'Oh, my God, Satya! What an amazing sight! So many baby rabbits!'

There they were with their white furry coats, red beady eyes, hopping around, up and down, toppling over one another!

'Satya, they are adorable.'

'Yeah, do you wanna touch them?'

'Oh, no, no, I'm scared, they are bursting with energy.'

'Arey, no, Kavya. Just sit here, this is Maxi, the gentlest one.'

Very gingerly, Kavya held Mr Maxi in one hand and started stroking him with the other.

Oh wow...super soft...softer than my teddy bear!

Satya chuckled and gave a bright smile.

'Oh, you lost your tooth. Same pinch!' said Kavya, giggling.

And they sat there talking nonstop, immersed in detailed conversations of what had happened in their lives; so much to catch up with, so much to share. They talked as if there was no comma or full stop to punctuate their chatter.

Satya was born and brought up in Kochipuram and was a brilliant student and a star athlete. His father Mr Rameshwar was a renowned lawyer as well as a landowner, making him one of the richest people in town. He was actively involved in local politics where he had a stronghold. His opinion and consent were always sought on all big and small decisions concerning the town, whether it was the Ganapati Mahotsav or a small temple pooja.

An influential man with a strong opinion, he had dreams of sending his son to the USA for his further studies once he turned 15, knowing well that no one else from this town had ever left the state for their education.

He would announce his decision every now and then, but poor Satya had other plans.

6. Satya

Satya was a 10-year-old who loved to spend most of his time in the lap of nature, either tramping about on nature trails or simply sitting for hours near a creek, observing and studying fish. He often fished them out and kept them in a huge cemented water tank on the terrace of his home. He felt that this way he could get a closer look whenever he needed to, and he couldn't do that at the creek.

The water tank was his laboratory, he studied the colour of their scales, their pattern of eating and activity levels vis-à-vis staying still and would Google other information and drown himself in research.

Till now, he had examined and identified more than 26 different varieties of fish in the creek water, and he attributed this high number to the quality of the water.

The water in Kochipuram was still the purest in the state. No factories were allowed around the perimeter of the town.

Satya's two Indie dogs shadowed him wherever he went – Muddy, a brown Indie, and Zuddu, a spotted mixed breed. When Zuddu was a pup, he fractured one of his limbs, and though it had healed now, it still impacted his ability to run fast.

Satya loved to spend time with Kavya as they both had a common connection.

Unlike boys of his age, Satya never wanted to play with the superhero figures like Superman or the Avengers. He led a gadget-free life and was amused by how his other schoolmates talked about new video games, etc. He shared everything with Kavya about his techie school friends and their obsession with fictional superheroes.

'And you know my classmate, Charvik, the one who has that electric jeep?' asked Satya.

'Oh, you mean "monster wheel"?' responded Kavya.

'Ya, that's what he calls it, "my monster wheel". He has changed his name from Charvik to Charz.'

'Like, seriously?' said Kavya in surprise.

'Ya, he feels Charvik doesn't suit his personality.'

'Oh, and what does Charz mean?'

'It's meaningless.'

'Oh, so things that are meaning less are more meaningful for them...'

'He is a huge Avengers fan and has "avengerized" everything from start to end. Charz's room has a huge 3D Avengers poster, he has a t-shirt with The Avengers embossed on it, and so many things like that.'

'Okay, forget all this. I am so hungry now, let's go down and grab a bite.'

'Really, hungry?' asked Satya.

'You think I'm joking?' Kavya responded.

'Okay, come.' He took her to the other end of the terrace.

'Wow, mulberries! And so many! We hardly get to eat any as they are only available in the market for such a short duration.' They pulled down a big branch laden with bunches of juicy mulberries and started gobbling them.

'Hey, just be careful when you eat them, okay? Just check the colour...is it looking fine?' asked Satya.

'Yeah, it's pink...and smells good.' Kavya began to devour the fruit, but Satya was being careful in eating them and checking them carefully from all sides before putting them into his mouth.

'Ewww! What's this? A worm? Yuck! Yucky, yucky!' She then threw up all the fruit she had.

She rushed downstairs and ran straight to Prabha Chachi.

'Arey, Kavya, what happened? Did you fall down? Why are you crying, Gudiya?'

'Water!' she gasped and pointed towards an earthen pot of water on the kitchen counter covered with a red cloth.

'Give her water immediately,' said Satya, running into the kitchen.

Prabha gently smoothed down her hair while Kavya guzzled the water down in loud gulps.

'He fed me a worm-infested mulberry...' Kavya whined, pointing to Satya.

'Arey, but why did you eat it?'

'I was so hungry, and it looked so yummy and delicious...' she trailed off.

'Oh, no, come and sit here. Look, what I am making for you,' Prabha said pointing to the payasam boiling in the pot.

'Arey, waah, Chachi. All my fault, I should never have listened to that crackpot!'

'Yeah, well, I told you. It's common sense, didn't you taste it in your mouth?' asked Satya.

'Ahem ahem, come here now, we need to talk seriously! How many times have we told you to let us treat that plant?' said his mother, pulling his ear.

'But, Maa, listen to me-'

'No, you listen to me, Satya. It's important to spray insecticide after every pruning season if you want to have worm-free fruits.'

'Maa, you know it's harmful to the tree, and tell me, what about the hundreds of birds that relish the sweet fruits of that tree? Do we need to place a signboard that says, "wash before eating" so that they are aware of the harmful effect?' argued Satya, opposing vehemently. 'And did I tell you there is a special guest residing in our mulberry tree? Baby owls! I have heard them hooting from there, which definitely means there are baby owls. Do you still want to treat it, Maa?' Satya delivered his tirade and darted out of the kitchen with his eyes misting up.

'Arey, Satya! Oh, this boy...'

'No, Chachi, I think he is right,' muttered Kavya in a remorseful voice.

'Arey, he's crazy. Stop thinking about him. Come here, taste this payasam. Be careful, it must be hot.'

'Looks delicious, Chachi,' said Kavya.

7. Evil Spirit

Satya's father, Mr Rameshwar, came home earlier than usual. He looked upset and angry. His driver carried his leather briefcase and black umbrella and ran after him looking down with an air of servility.

Prabha greeted him with her customary smile and the standard question of the past 16 years, 'How was your day?'

Mr Rameshwar looked at Prabha and sighed deeply. He opened the top button of his shirt, rubbed the back of his neck, and muttered out of frustration under his breath.

Prabha had a telepathic connection with her husband. She instinctively realised that something bad had happened. She looked at Tilakas Das, their driver, and raised her eyebrows questioningly. He hung his head and went outside, refusing to meet her eyes.

Prabha approached Mr Rameshwar in a composed manner and enquired why he was so agitated and allowed his blood pressure to rise over a seemingly trivial issue.

'Calm down, have this.' She gave him a glass of water infused with the essence of jasmine, rose petals, and lemon drops.

He sipped it slowly, let out a groan, and settled down on the teak wood sofa which was large enough to seat five people at a time.

He held Prabha's hand and said, 'I lost the election, Prabha. For the first time in fifteen years, I feel like a failure...'

Prabha knew how important this election was for her husband and she could understand what he was going through.

'But, how?'

'I don't know, how! Seems like some bad luck; like someone's evil eye is on our house,'

saying this he got up and went straight to his bedroom.

Bad luck in my house? How is that possible?

Prabha could not sleep that night as the question of bad luck remained on her mind constantly. She kept thinking of the different ways she could use to ward off bad luck if at all it was present. And suddenly, a thought crossed her mind – *is it because of those owls?*

Oh, no, no...How foolish is my son to harbour the presence of evil in my house! I will speak to Pandit ji tomorrow.

Oh, God! Please, keep your hand on us.

She tossed and turned but still couldn't sleep. She got up from her bed and slowly walked towards the window. Gently, she moved the curtain aside, opened the window, placed her trembling hand on the window pane, and leaned outside to see if there was any sign of some bad omen. She looked around fearfully and bravely locked her gaze on the giant mulberry tree. She peered intently and tried to make out images in the dark. There was a strong wind blowing and every branch and leaf of the tree was swaying in the wind; it was as if the entire tree had come to life and was dancing to its own beat.

Prabha quickly rushed back to her bed after closing all the windows and curtains firmly this time. She was breathing heavily, trying to believe that what she had just seen was not true.

The next morning, Prabha was shivering with a fever and sweating in a very unusual way.

Sitting next to her was Savitri, mopping her forehead with a cold towel. She said, 'I hope what you saw yesterday was not true, but still, these things don't go easily without taking something precious from the family.'

'What are you saying, Savitri?' asked Prabha in a stressed voice.

'Yes, Didi, I think you must get rid of that tree. I believe that is the only way to completely ward off the evil shadow that is hovering over us.' So saying, she clutched a locket around her neck which had the image of Lord Hanuman stamped on it.

'You are right, Savitri, that tree is evil,' Prabha said.

She made up her mind. *We will get rid of the evil spirit as soon as possible.*

'You go and call Sahib.'

'Didi, think about it. Satya Baba may not approve of this decision.'

'You do as I say.'

After some time, Mr Rameshwar entered the room. He enquired about Prabha's health and sat on the wooden rocking chair located on the other side of the bed. He took out his reading glasses and unfolded the newspaper he held in his hand.

Prabha silently gestured to Savitri to go and make some tea for them.

'Listen, I need to talk to you about something important.'

'Hmm.'

'Are you listening?'

'Hmm, tell me,' Mr Rameshwar said, his face hidden behind the newspaper.

'I said something important and you seem to be the least bit interested.'

'Arey, tell, baba. I am listening...'

'I know why all this has happened.'

'What happened?'

'Your election results.'

'Now, don't lecture me on this, Prabha, I am already pissed.'

'No, baba, I mean I know why this has happened...listen na...'

Mr Rameshwar lowered the newspaper and leaned towards her to hear the big secret.

'We have an evil shadow hovering over the family.'

'A what?'

'Come closer, I can't shout. Something happened yesterday that was exceptional. You have never lost the elections, but you lost this time!' she said triumphantly and continued. 'That was just a warning...We have an evil spirit lurking over us!'

'Oh, please, Prabha...Stop it.'

'Come closer, do you think with this high fever, I am in any mood to joke with you?'

'What are you saying, Prabha?'

'I saw it yesterday...with my own eyes.'

'What?' He took off his glasses and sat closer. 'Really?'

Prabha leaned towards him and whispered in his ear. Mr Rameshwar looked at her and said, 'Oh, God, please have mercy on our family.' He put his palms together in supplication. Prabha also joined her hands together and muttered the same appeal under her breath.

'The presence of an owl is worse than any other evil, and now she has also laid eggs. She is in no mood to go, do you understand? We need to act fast,' said Prabha.

'You are right,' said Mr Rameshwar. 'Let's get rid of the tree.'

'Yes, as soon as possible.'

Mr Rameshwar went out of the room and immediately ordered his driver to call someone from the forest reservation authority to cut the tree down and get rid of the nest. Within an hour, the decade-old tree was chopped into pieces.

The whole courtyard was littered with branches and leaves. The mighty tree which had stood for years spreading its cool shade during the scorching summers now lay in a broken heap. Crushed mulberries lay strewn over the verandah, oozing their red juice as if to show that the tree was bleeding profusely. Streams of ants were marching to savour this unexpected bounty, perhaps knowing that this would be their last treat here.

An enormous tree had fallen flat. The chirping of the birds that could be heard from a kilometre away was now silenced because there was no place for them here anymore. Satya was completely unaware of this mishap as he played blissfully in Kavya's house. Kavya's mother brought two glasses of milk.

'Here you go, little champs,' said Mrs Murthy.

Kavya was very fond of milk and could have it any time of the day as a milky treat, before or after a meal.

'Hey, Satya, look what I have,' she said, showing him a small pack of glucose biscuits.

Satya cheerfully said, 'Oh, I was so missing them! Here, give them to me quickly.'

'Hello, we need to share...' Kavya hastily pulled her hand back and took out her pencil box to use it as a makeshift hammer. She then started crushing the biscuits inside the packet until they turned to powder.

She poured half the crumbs into Satya's milk and the rest into hers and made a slurry.

'Mmm...yummy!'

They relished every last drop of it and licked their glasses clean. Using their fingers, they scraped off any errant blobs that were stuck to the sides and pushed them into their mouths as they inverted the glass over their mouths and willed the last drops to trickle down the sides and fall onto their tongues.

'Oh, I'm so full!'

'Me too, and it is so creamy.'

Both children sighed contentedly as they licked their lips and sat back in satisfaction.

8. The Mulberry Tree

Satya bid farewell to Kavya and headed home as he wanted to be there before his father got back; an unwritten law that was followed by everyone. Meal times were family time and all meals had to be eaten together at a specified time; if not, one may end up sacrificing their food for the inefficiency of not planning one's time effectively.

Satya took off his slippers outside his house and then went in to wash his hands and feet. He saw people going out with bundles of chopped logs on their heads. He rushed in and couldn't believe his eyes at the sight he saw.

His old mulberry tree, which he believed would be there to stand tall for eternity, was slain down in pieces.

He yelled out to his mother in a desperate voice.

'Maa, our tree! What happened?' asked Satya, his voice heavy with pain.

'It was necessary, and you should be happy that your family is safe from the shadow of the evil spirit,' replied Prabha.

'What? Maa, you did this? What's wrong with you, Maa? How could you just kill it? Baba, is it true? You chopped down my tree?'

'Satya, stop being melodramatic, it was just a tree,' said Mr Rameshwar in a stern voice.

The mulberry tree which yielded the sweetest and juiciest little fruits was planted by Satya's grandfather when he was born. The tree was like a blessing from his grandfather and Satya had nurtured it since he was five.

He loved to spend time sitting on the branches, climbing up and down the trunk. His grandfather was no more but he could feel his happy energy whenever he spent time with his old friend.

In this distressed state, a thought crossed his mind – *what about the owls?*

He asked Savitri and she responded, 'What owl? I don't know, maybe they flew away...that's what they do. Good thing Didi decided to have the tree cut. I had to waste my whole day cleaning these bird droppings...it was so painful. Now, there will be no one to dirty our verandah.' She went about her work prattling non-stop and nodded her head wisely. 'There was negative energy coming from the tree and Didi took swift action.'

Satya looked around in disbelief. He ran up to the terrace and hooted softly, calling out to the poor owlets. He cried, then wiped his tears and kept calling out for them.

But he did not get a reply.

'They have left me, they have left me,' wailed Satya and crawled into the corner of the terrace, weeping in pain and helplessness.

The next morning Satya slept till late. And though he was awake, he didn't want to get out of bed. He hid his face behind another pillow trying to block out the bright sunshine that was streaming through his window.

Satya was bewildered by the sudden brightness that lit up his bedroom and unable to go back to sleep, he flung off his blanket and looked all around him his room. He faced east and was now suddenly facing the gull glory of the Sun god. He wondered where this light was coming from and when he looked towards the window, he got his answer. The tree which had stood tall for a decade was now not there to prevent the sharp rays of the sun from entering the room. They streamed in fearlessly as there was no one to obstruct their passage. He looked at the sunbeams and noticed small particles of dust dancing about, perhaps to their own melodies. They looked amazing, completely unaware of the fact that this was one of the gloomiest mornings for Satya.

He had learned a critical life lesson here. Life marches on whether you choose to move on or stay behind locked in the past. Life is not something that can be tuned or turned to the way we want it.

He got out of bed and went straight to the bathroom. He wore a maroon half-sleeved shirt and full pants and combed his hair neatly taking care to part it on the side. He stood in front of the mirror and stared back at his reflection. His eyes were still red, but he had made up his mind to announce his decision to his parents. He knew his father would be very happy for him, but this time, it was more for himself.

Satya skipped down the stairs and looked around. The usual morning routines were happening; Prabha was sitting with Savitri on the verandah instructing her on how she should wash the rice, Mr Rameshwar had his face buried in the newspaper and steam was emitting from the freshly brewed cup of coffee that he was holding in his hand.

Satya went up to Mr Rameshwar and touched his feet and deferentially wished him good morning. Mr Rameshwar nodded his head twice and sipped the piping hot coffee.

'Baba, when can I go to boarding school?' Satya asked.

Mr Rameshwar looked up from his paper with an astonished expression on his face.

'Yes, Baba, I am now ready to go.'

He couldn't believe what he had just heard.

'Oh, come here, Satya.' He held out his hand and hugged him.

'I am so glad you finally agreed. It has been my dream to see my child graduate from such a prestigious institution.'

'Can I join from this academic year?' asked Satya with an expressionless face.

Prabha, who was sitting some distance away, stood up adjusting her saree.

'What? This academic year? No, no, he can't go that early. He is too young to join a boarding school!' said Prabha, looking at her husband with misty eyes.

With determination stamped across his face, Satya said, 'I need to join soon, I can't miss any more years.'

'Yes, yes, you are right, I will call the school authorities to expedite the procedure. I am so happy today.'

Prabha covered her mouth with her saree, and with her eyes brimming over in disbelief.

'It's a happy occasion, Prabha, please be strong. I am sure Satya will make us proud one day.'

Prabha ran into the kitchen and cried uncontrollably.

Satya, on the other hand, looked composed as he stood there without any expression. He looked at the empty courtyard. Everything looked just the same, except that the tree wasn't there anymore. He could see himself playing under the tree, monkeying around and jumping from one branch to the other. A lone tear rolled down his cheek and he hastily wiped it away before anyone saw it.

9. Bitter and Sweet Experiences

As you embark on a new journey, you fill your luggage with everything necessary. The same goes for when you return from that journey, but instead of loading your bags, you load your mind and heart with new experiences, unforgettable memories, and sweet acquaintances with new people. Such is the beauty of any journey – it enriches your life and makes it more sensitive and meaningful.

After a bittersweet experience, Kavya returned to her city.

With a new session, new class, and a new set of books and stationery awaiting her, it didn't take Kavya much time to put her hometown in the back of her mind and switch to regular city life. Subconsciously, however, Kochipuram had imprinted deeply on her personality this time.

10. Back to School

'Okay, children, okay, quiet now!' said Mrs Pinto, Kavya's class teacher. 'We need to decide and submit our suggestions before the weekend.'

'For what, Madam?' asked the class in chorus.

'Shhh, softly, there is a class going on next door,' Mrs Pinto admonished them in her strong British accent. 'The annual excursion. Please, submit your responses by the end of the day or latest by Friday. What would you prefer, a visit to the zoo, the botanical gardens, or the planetarium?'

'Ma'am, zoo! Please, ma'am, please!'

'Not like this. Submit your response on a piece of paper, and we will decide on the place chosen unanimously.'

There was a sudden buzz as the children started discussing the various options. A few bossy ones were trying to influence the others to get a maximum vote for the zoo.

'Excuse me, ma'am?'

'Yes, Kavya,' said Mrs Pinto.

'Can we consider some other options also?'

'Where else would you like to go?'

'Like, could we consider an animal rescue park – Spandhan?'

Mrs Pinto raised her head and lifted her glasses, placing them on her head.

'Could you explain a bit further?' said Mrs Pinto authoritatively.

'Ma'am, for the last six months I have been studying cruelty towards birds and animals. Hundreds of rescued birds have lost their vision, and some have lost a wing to a poacher, etc. We need to sensitise our society towards these cruel deeds. Through these trips, we will learn how to care for nature and respect all living creatures. This is my suggestion,' Kavya concluded.

'I'm okay with whatever the majority says. But one thing is for sure, I am definitely going to visit this place with my family,' said Mrs Pinto with a smile.

As soon as the teacher left, the class gathered around Kavya, enquiring more about this place.

'How can anyone be cruel to little birds?' asked Saisha, who was one of the most intelligent students in the class with a fair complexion, bespectacled and petite.

'I think it's a great opportunity for all of us, and a visit here will be instrumental in teaching us the correct art and science of living in tune with nature,' Kavya continued.

'Hmm, I agree with Kavya,' said Bhaskar, who was very fond of animals.

'Well, it's a kind of zoo. The only difference is that the animals here were once abused and are kept and cared for until they are well enough to go back to their natural habitat, unlike other commercial zoos where they are forced to spend their entire lives in captivity,' explained Kavya.

'How true!' said Saisha. 'Count me in.'

'Me too!' said Bhaskar.

And so, the majority of the class voted for Spandhan.

'Great then,' said Mrs Pinto. '6 October. Sunday. Fixed for Spandhan. But I need a signed acknowledgement from your parents.'

11. Field Trip

The week couldn't go past fast enough, but like anything worth waiting for, the day finally arrived – the most awaited day of the year – The Annual Field Trip.

The children were super excited about their excursion. A great deal of planning was going on. On one hand, the children were deciding amongst themselves who would bring what treats – jujubes, chewing gums, orange suckles, wafers, and fruit juices; everyone chipped in happily as the excitement was threatening to brim over. On the other hand, and on a more official level, the teachers were repeating instructions for the children to follow school protocol – come in your school uniform, don't forget your ID cards, and bring your water bottles and mini snack boxes.

Finally, the day arrived! A yellow air-conditioned bus was parked under the tree.

The teachers and school staff were busy dictating last-minute dos and don'ts to the driver and the caretaker. Food and water cartons were being loaded into the bus. Karan saw the small juice packs being loaded onto the bus. He nudged Kavya and pointed towards the juice, and they both giggled in sheer joy.

The children were all standing in a queue, anxiously waiting to board the bus. Mrs Pinto stood at the entrance with an attendance roster in her hand. Her cheeks were turning red and drops of sweat were beginning to settle on her forehead. The inspection of the bus was carried out by the technician to avoid any last-minute technical glitches. He came out of the bus with his shirt soaked to the skin in sweat and banged on the side to indicate – 'All OK'.

Once the all-ok signal was given, the children started boarding the bus. Mrs Pinto made sure everyone walked in single file and everyone could hear her snapping out instructions – no pushing, stick to the line, don't dawdle!

As the saying goes, the journey is always more interesting than the destination. The children made sure that these three hours were the most memorable of their lives!

The brainiacs occupied the front rows, as they were more concerned about impressing the teacher with their good manners rather than joining the mad party at the back of the bus.

Kavya and her gang occupied the middle rows. Karan made a paper ball and chucked it at Kavya. Very soon, Saisha and Neha joined the fray and started throwing paper balls at each other. The children sitting in the front were singing songs, totally unaware of the chaos happening in the back. And then, accidentally, a paper ball that was targeted at Rini landed on Mrs Pinto! Well, that was the last round of that amusing game. She saw Karan chucking it and immediately had him exchange places with another boy in the front row.

Poor Karan ended up having to endure his bus ride singing songs with the chorus girls.

After some time, refreshments were served, and the sports teacher who accompanied the children on all trips instructed them to take one packet and pass the box to the next. For the next five minutes, there was complete silence in the bus and just the sound of food packets being passed around could be heard.

Soon, the children were instructed to pack their bags and be ready to get off as they were about to reach their destination.

12. Trip to Spandhan

'Good morning!' said Mr Albert in a cheerful voice, reciprocated immediately by the children. Mr Albert was the founder of this rehabilitation initiative.

'So, let me brief you about Spandhan first. It's a wildlife rehabilitation initiative for the treatment and care of injured, orphaned, or sick birds and animals so that they can be released into the wild. Our motto is "It's Our Planet Too!" Of course, even the smallest living being has a right to live freely and we have no right to make this world a museum. Human beings have always wanted to possess whatever they liked, this has been their problem from the beginning of evolution.

So, the park is spread over a total area of twenty acres. We have forty-two flapshell turtles, and more than three hundred parrots. Peacocks that we saved from the clutches of poachers who used to kill these beautiful birds for their feathers, at least twenty-one...'

This brought a round of applause from the children.

'...a thousand tiny colourful birds that fly around freely. Wait, wait, wait, the list is long...' said Mr Albert enunciating each word, indicative of the great sense of pride in the work that he was doing.

'Asian bears and eighteen sloth bears that were rescued from the dancing bear trade, we have Jambi and her rescued family.'

'Wow!' exclaimed the children.

'Do they roam around freely?' asked Saisha curiously.

'Hahaha!' laughed Mr Albert. 'Yes, freely, but in their designated enclosures ensuring that they don't disturb their neighbours.'

'Oh, that's smart,' said Kavya.

'No, it's just being sensitive. They are sensitive towards their surroundings by not polluting them and caring for their ecosystem. We, humans, need to learn the art of living by watching these tiny animals.'

'Oh, look, an anthill!'

'Ah, yes, come close, all of you. I will tell you some very interesting facts about this ordinary-looking anthill. First of all,' continued Mr Albert, 'humans are not the only creatures who build awe-inspiring homes. A lot of animals and birds put in a great deal of effort in creating structures like this.

'Now, this ant castle is an inspiration for all of us. This may appear to be a very normal muddy structure from the outside but if you look at the inner mechanism of this anthill, it's extremely complex and baffling. It has many tunnels and chambers of varying sizes. These tunnels connect to different chambers in a manner that even an expert maze runner would have a difficult time finding his way out. Each chamber in the anthill has different nurseries for the young ones, called grubs. Some chambers serve as storage rooms for storing food, and even though worker ants spend most of their time searching for food, they have their own reserved quarters to rest.'

'Now, the question you may all ask is – why do they make a hill?' continued Mr Albert. 'Anyone?'

'Because they want to stay together,' said Zara hesitantly in her innocent voice.

'How sweet! We all indeed want to stay together as a family, but here they have one more purpose. Ants make a hill to keep the larvae of their queen safe. And it's interesting to note that a worker ant will move the larvae into the room nearest to the top of the anthill to keep it warm during the day. At night, they will move them to a lower chamber to keep them safe.'

'Wow! That's pretty cool.'

'Smart ants.'

'Yes, that's why I call it an ant castle. On the surface, they might look like tiny crawling insects, but if you observe them closely, you will learn that they are amongst the most hardworking ones who work tirelessly, day and night, like real soldiers. Every living creature on this planet is an inspiration in itself. So, children, there are many things that we can learn from ants. Any guesses?'

'Hard work!' suggested one child.

'Right! Hard work is important. Anything else?'

'We can learn about teamwork and coordination,' said another.

'There you go! That's a great one. Say, for example, Mrs Pinto had to ask you to make a line and walk in a single file. I am sure Mrs Pinto knows how hoarse her throat will be to get you to do this...'

Mrs Pinto shrugged her shoulders helplessly and smiled.

'And another marvellous thing about ants is that they are great planners. They prepare their food in summer because they know that winter will bring a scarcity of food. They are great team players. If a few ants in the colony are infected by a fungal disease, they spread the disease throughout the colony, by licking it off one another and spreading it around as much as possible and in the process diluting the impact of the disease. This ensures that each ant can then fight it off with its individual immune system.'

'Wow, they are real heroes,' chorused the children, clapping in admiration of how smart ants were.

'How do you know so much about ant colonies and what the inside looks like? I have always wondered how it looks from the inside,' asked Bhaskar, who seemed very impressed with the vast amount of information about this magnificent creature.

'Well, if you want to study them closely, you can always have a formicarium or ant farm, which is designed primarily for the study of ant colonies and their behaviour. By the way, a person who studies ant behaviour is called a myrmecologist. That's for your record.'

They all mumbled back, 'Myrmecol... myrmecologist...'

'Okay, here's one more very interesting fact about Mr Ant 🐜. Do you know how they communicate?'

'Hmm...they don't make a sound for sure.'

'Any guesses?'

'With their eyes,' said Subho.

'Eyes...Can you talk with your eyes.?'

'Yeah, I do sometimes. Like, when I am angry, I make my eyes really big and when I see something and feel greedy about it my eyes shine and sparkle, and if I have a question to ask I stare and lift my eyebrows up and down like this.'

All the children burst into laughter at Subho's clownish answer.

'Well done, Subho, it was indeed an entertaining act but unfortunately, ants don't have as expressive a face as you. Mr Ant uses its feelers or antennae to talk to other ants. If you watch those lines of ants marching up and down, you will notice that they meet and greet each other constantly. C'mon, let's all make antennas...C'mon, c'mon!'

'Yeah, like this, with fingers on your heads and rolled on the top. Now, come on, pass on the message.'

'What's the message, sir?'

'The message is I am very happy and positive.'

There was the sound of children giggling and joking, busy as ants as they went about playing and enjoying their day.

'Now, that's a lot of information,' said Dhruv, huffing and puffing. He had pushed the peak of his blue and black cap to the back of his head, over his neck.

'Oh, I think the young man is a little bored. I have something that can shoo away your boredom in a minute. Alright, everyone, come closer.'

There were layers of dry leaves underfoot. Any little movement by the children resulted in a delicious crunching sound; a sound that they all loved. All the children stood around Mr Albert, stomping on dry leaves, and enjoying the sound of the crackle.

'So, Captain Dhruv, you look the bravest of them all, is that true?' asked Mr Albert.

'Oh, of course,' he said, shrugging his shoulders.

'So, I want you to meet my best friend. Would you like to?'

'Yeah, you mean your elephant?'

'Oh, no, not that big a friend,' said Mr Albert.

'Oh, ya, why not?'

All the children were yelling in the background saying they wanted to meet...

'Shhh! Okay, just close your eyes and open them when I call out your name.'

Mr Albert signalled all the kids to be quiet. He winked and assured them of a great surprise. They were giggling and nudging each other to keep mum. Very quickly, Mr Albert put his hand into his right pocket and pulled out his best buddy, a giant tarantula! He then held it up in front of Dhruv's face saying, 'My Tula is saying "Hello, Dhruv!"'

Dhruv opened his eyes like a cool dude and saw a giant hairy spider right in front of his face!

He let out a mighty scream – so loud that you could see all of his teeth.

'Hey, that must be poisonous,' enquired Kavya.

'No, dear, not all scary-looking spiders are harmful. Unfortunately, these are exotic pets for a few callous people who buy them without actually being aware of their special needs, and this one landed up here with me,' said Mr Albert, raising his brows.

'But I think we are friends, right, Tula?' The spider happily crawled up his arm, resting back in his pocket.

'Wow that was amazing, I am totally awake now,' giggled Dhruv, trying to hide a lost canine tooth.

'Oh, that actually looks like the hideout of a cavity nester,' said Mr Albert.

'Now, what is that? asked Dhruv.

'You know, these birds that use natural cavities or excavate cavities in the tree as their nests...like woodpeckers, owls, and yes, also parrots – they are all cavity nesters.' The children now felt smug and proud of this new prestigious title of missing teeth instead of considering them only "lost tooth holes".'

The children fell into a single file as they followed Mr Albert, walking on fresh green trails, nature unfolding before their eyes in all its pristine and untouched beauty. This was verily a road-to-Damascus experience for all of them. It was soothing not just to their eyes, but it was also bringing purity to their thoughts. With curiosity in mind, the little crusaders followed Mr Albert hastily.

Mr Albert was a strong young man with a ruddy complexion and muscular physique. He was born in his ancestral house in a small village near the coastal belt but soon moved to Phuket, a beautiful island in Thailand, famous for its tropical beaches.

Since his father worked there as a forest tour guide, Mr Albert spent his childhood growing up in a wildlife corridor. He had seen his father dedicate his entire life to animals and the same was ingrained in his blood. It was his father's dream to establish a wildlife conservation park. So, after completing his formal education, Mr Albert returned to his hometown with the sole purpose of fulfilling his father's dream. Therefore, Spandhan was established in his memory to educate people about how they should treat animals and bring about a lasting change in society.

Under the pretext of showing love and affection, people buy these birds and animals without even bothering to learn about their life cycles or being concerned about their social needs. And once they lose interest or are unable to handle these responsibilities any further, they abandon them.

If time permitted, Mr Albert and his team of volunteers would love to knock on every door and enlighten people on how they were harming nature by keeping her creatures locked up and confined. He and his passionate team of volunteers worked day and night intending to free every bird locked in a cage and yearning to fly free. They shouted out to society as a whole to boycott any kind of animal abuse.

Soon, it was noon.

'I think we should have a small meal break now, you children must be hungry,' suggested Mr Albert.

'Umm I don't know about the children, but I sure am very hungry,' said Mrs Pinto.

The children lined up to wash their hands from a hand pump installed in the park. This turned into the centre of attraction for the children who may have seen and read about it but were actually using it for the first time. Pushing and pumping the long handle, watching a thick stream of cool water gush out brought them untold joy, a joy that was a rarity to see in this world of emoticons; where hearty laughter had turned into an "LOL" and the warmth of human touch was replaced by an "I am just a call away".

Mucking about in the dirt, unmindful of consequences in a childlike way, tramping about in the open park, puffing and panting in the heat, the children's cheeks were flushed red like Kashmiri apples. They were asked to settle down under the giant banyan tree, which was one of the oldest trees in the park. Freshly cooked food was served with a lot of love and affection. They ate to their heart's content and played about tracing snails and hopping after grasshoppers.

Mr Albert came and sat next to Kavya and thanked her for bringing the children. He believed in grassroots education and that children were the foundation of that change.

'Oh, Mr Albert, you know I am an ardent follower and how passionate I am about these creatures. We need to educate our society, and I think they are now ready to see the other end of Spandhan.' So saying, Kavya stood up to make an announcement, her eyes turning misty.

'Friends, I hope you have enjoyed your visit so far.'

'It's mind-boggling!' screamed Ayyan from the other end with all the others joining in.

'But from here, we will now visit another part of Spandhan. I know it's going to be tough for you all as it will be your first face-off with reality. Here, you will witness how abhorrent and monstrous human beings can be towards these innocent creatures,' concluded Kavya.

'Only the brave of heart can walk past this bridge,' said Mr Albert in a commanding voice.

The children picked themselves up and slowly moved towards the other part of Spandhan. As they walked through this bit of the park, they noticed something strange in the first containment zone, though the birds were kept in an open cage, none of them were flying out. As they moved ahead, they saw many colourful nests hanging in a cluster of bamboo trees with hundreds of colourful birds cramped together, almost as if they were scared of moving far from their nests.

A continuous flutter of wings and the buzzing of birds were coming from that tree and as Mr Albert was showing them the variety of love birds staying in a mini bamboo forest, a small red bird came and sat on Mr Albert's shoulder.

'Ah, you angel! isn't she beautiful?' he asked the children, holding her by her claws.

'Absolutely wonderful!' they all responded.

'But this beauty of hers is her greatest enemy.'

'What do you mean, Mr Albert?' asked Saisha in a concerned tone.

'She is blind, like all the other birds living in the mini bamboo forest, only the babies who are born here can see. They have adapted to these surroundings and have made this bamboo forest their home.'

'How come they are blind?' asked Mrs Pinto innocently.

'Poachers. Poachers make them blind. That's their technique for catching the birds. To catch the birds in the wild, the hunters use two of them as bait and gouge out their eyes. These blind and wounded birds are then left on a tarp, where they cry out for help. Soon hundreds of birds flock down to help. As they fly down, the hunters throw a net over them and capture them. The smugglers capture around a hundred birds at a time and then transport them to different countries, usually stuffed into small boxes and left without food and water for days. They suffer from captivity stress, severe dehydration, trauma, infections, and injuries due to travel and transportation in inhuman conditions.

'The data says that 60 per cent of the birds poached will die in the process, but the ones that do survive cover the cost in sales. Approximately, only one in ten smuggled birds survives,' explained Mr Albert.

'Oh, that's awful! How can they make the poor bird blind?'

'It is unfortunate but that is the fact.'

The children looked at the bamboo clumps and saw that hundreds of birds were merrily chirping and chattering with each other.

'These little birds are busy interacting with each other and still happy with their sightless life, do you know why? Because they are together. Isolating them is a crime. Birds are social animals. They fly together as a flock and are comfortable in each other's companionship.'

'Do you know what happens to a bird when is kept in isolation? Life in a cage is like a death sentence! Can you imagine yourself being confined to one room for your entire life, even the very thought is scary! So, just think of the plight of these poor helpless birds who are punished for their lifetime; far from their homes, away from their loved ones, confined to cramped cages where even fluttering their wings is a challenge, let alone flying a few inches.'

'Never tamper with Mother Nature. Have you heard the story of the mouse and the lion? Man is the mouse here. He plays with nature, tampers with ecosystems, carries out indiscriminate chopping of trees, unruly excavations, unplanned mining...the list is endless. What else can you expect but landslides, floods, droughts, and other natural calamities? It's nature's way of retaliating.'

'Is no one in this world bothered about these innocent animals?' asked a child from the crowd in a hoarse voice.

'Fortunately, yes. There are people and organisations in support of these little angels. Hope you have heard of NGOs like People for Animals, World Organisation for Animal Health, PETA (People for the Ethical Treatment of Animals), and RAWW (Resqink Association for Wildlife Welfare). They have dedicated their entire lives to conserving these fabulous creatures and optimising their efforts to keep them happy and alive in their natural habitat.'

Spending a day in Spandhan was a life-changing experience for the children. It touched their hearts, and their entire outlook towards life changed as they learnt many life lessons.

As the sun was beginning to set, the heat of the day also gave way to a cooler and calmer evening. Mrs Pinto shared a brief message of commendation for their hard work and gratitude for their patience, with the entire team of Spandhan. There was a special mention of Mr Albert for taking so much time and effort in answering all the questions of the inquisitive children.

'It's our pleasure to have these wonderful young boys and girls at our place. I am sure they will grow up into responsible and compassionate adults in our country. Before I forget, here is a small token of appreciation for all our young guests.'

Mr Albert signalled his staff to distribute small wrapped gifts.

'Oh, thank you, Mr Albert, that's so thoughtful of you!' said Kavya.

'You are most welcome, young lady.'

Kavya opened her pack and found small birds made out of a bamboo leaf. 'So beautiful!' exclaimed Kavya.

'I'm glad you liked your gift.'

Tired but cheerful, the children boarded the bus, slowly and politely making way for each other; it was obvious that they had taken Mr Albert's statement of "be a responsible citizen" very seriously. Mrs Pinto checked against her attendance roster to be double sure that they had not left anyone behind. This time, there was no chatter in the bus. They all settled down quietly, lost in their thoughts. They were amazed at how much life could prosper without human interference.

13. Sunday Funday

Sunday – the best day of the week was here. There was no rush in Mrs Murthy's kitchen. Coffee was brewing on one stove, while all the others were enjoying a break from the weekday breakfast rush; no strident whistles from the pressure cooker, no smoky tempering, just the warm aroma of fresh coffee brewing. Mrs Murthy was engaged in her hair care ritual and grinding *methi* seeds that she had soaked the night before.

Mr Murthy who was back from a week-long official tour was relaxing in his rocking chair, his fingers beating a rhythmic tattoo on the arms of the wooden rocker, the golden rings on all four fingers were adding a beat of their own to the impromptu tune. A radio was playing classical Carnatic music in the background.

Mrs Murthy stepped out into the courtyard, the sound of her glass bangles tinkling, and announced, 'Coffee!'

Mr Murthy took the cup and enquired about the morning newspaper. 'Why does he come so late?' he asked no one in particular, grumbling under his breath and expressing his disappointment as he sipped the piping hot coffee.

Kavya crept up to her father and covered his eyes with her soft pudgy hands.

'Peekaboo!' shrieked Kavya in her father's ear.

'Oh, who is this naughty girl? Let me guess! Let me guess!'

'Good morning, Baba. When did you come, Baba?'

'Oh, my baby Kavi, last night.'

'But why didn't you wake me up?'

'Oh, no, Kavya, it was very late. You were fast asleep.'

'Bad bad bad!' she admonished him. 'And have you brought my favourite treat?'

'Go check it out. It's in the kitchen.'

She ran to the kitchen and picked up her parcel packed in a newspaper, hastily tearing off the wrapper before she devoured some of the sweets.

For a moment, she closed her eyes and savoured the sweetness that filled her mouth.

Hmmm, yummy. She came running out with her mouth full and kissed her father.

'It's so good, Baba,' crumbs fell out of her mouth as she tried to speak and sat next to him. Her mother motioned her not to speak with her mouth full.

'Oh, sorry.'

Kavya took the last bite and started repacking it in the newspaper.

How strange, the newspaper might feel. The most treasured thing in the morning becomes trash in the evening, she thought.

The picture of a huge colourful bird featured in the "Our City" section of the paper caught her attention.

She came up to her Baba, pointed to the picture, and asked curiously, 'Is this real, Baba?'

Mr Murthy reached for his spectacles and read the paper before nodding his head.

He quickly read a few lines and said that the article was about some people from her school – Mt Halton School. It appeared that they had imported a macaw from some region of America.

She grabbed the piece of paper and started reading it quickly. She couldn't believe her eyes that it was an interview with her principal.

'Kids love to be around nature and these creatures bring positive energy to our little ones who often feel down while coming to school. This beautiful creature has been imported from Central America and we have waited for months to bring this majestic bird into our family. I am sure all the children will be waiting eagerly to get their first glimpse of the new addition.'

'Baba, did you see this? Wow! I am desperate to see it.'

She hugged her father and ran upstairs to her room with the page in her hand. Kavya sat at her study table and admired the beauty of the innocent bird, its long tail, colourful plumage, and rounded blue beak. She cut the picture out and pinned it on her soft board. She opened her computer and began reading about the macaw birds. She browsed the internet reading about how they were kept as a pet, what they liked to eat, what their behaviour was like, and their life span.

She eagerly waited for the day to end.

The next morning, as Kavya entered the school, she saw a huge rush circling the newly bought pet. With ogling eyes, she looked at the bird and her heart raced as she went closer to it.

The bird stood still, not making any movement, not even blinking its eye. It was hard to believe that it was a living bird. Kavya looked at the cage; it was a huge golden cage, with a small hanging bottle for water, and trays of different feeds like corn, green beans, and some other seeds sprinkled on the floor of the cage. She desperately wanted to befriend the bird and strongly believed that there was a connection between the two of them. She wanted to caress the bird and stroke its feathers. Kavya did indeed make some throaty sounds to lure the bird but failed to catch its attention. She remembered her old friend Captain, how she used to feed him crispy corn and caress him with love and affection.

Suddenly, she spotted an earthworm in a nearby potted plant. She watched it attentively as it was burrowing down into the soil; there were multiple wormholes around it.

'Looks like he is not alone,' muttered Kavya.

She looked back at the parrot's cage and asked it innocently, 'Want one?' Kavya frantically searched for a twig and found one in the fence nearby. Armed with the twig, she tried to pick up a wriggly squirmy worm. Eventually, she managed to lure one onto the stick and got it to wrap itself around.

She took a firm hold of the stick and presented the warm treat to the bird.

'Here you go, birdie. I am sure you are missing this,' saying this, she pushed the worm close to the bird's face.

The poor bird who was trapped in an enclosure so small that it could barely stretch its wings, was sad and scared and couldn't understand this sudden encroachment of its personal space.

It let out a loud scream, accompanied by a lot of distraught pacing in the cramped cage.

The unusual squawking startled Kavya. She ran away, dropping the twig inside the cage. With her heart racing, she ran straight to her classroom.

The children were sitting around in small groups of twos or threes, a few were in a big group having separate discussions about the macaw bird.

Kavya settled down in her seat, quietly hoping that the others had not seen what had just happened. She looked up and took a deep breath; everyone was busy now with their own home assignments & lectures but Kavya was still self-absorbed.

It was now recess time. A few children went outside to play, while others sat in the group, chatting and sharing food. Half-heartedly, Kavya took out her lunch box, shook it a bit, and said, 'Idli again.' She guessed right. Snowy white idlis popped out. She broke off a piece, dunked it in the coconut chutney, and ate it mindlessly.

The bell rang, and teachers took their classes and left. Everything was going as per schedule. Finally, the last bell rang, signalling the end of school for the day.

Kavya pushed her books back into her bag, buckled it down, and just wanted to check on the macaw one last time as she walked out of the classroom.

She went back to the small park area designated as a nursery for plants, and to her surprise, the bird stood motionless as if there was no life left in it. Its red eyes seemed to be cast in stone staring fixedly at one place. She wondered if it had eaten or drunk anything the whole day. She hung her bag on her shoulder and came closer to the cage. And like the wonder of wonders, the worm was no longer there!

Had the bird eaten it? Or had it let it go?

She presumed that her treat had been accepted by her new friend, and happy with her first move, she left school planning her next date with the bird.

14. Kavya and the Macaw

It was a lazy afternoon when the heat from the sun had managed to crawl into all the nooks and crannies of the surroundings and made the air around oppressively heavy with haze. Little Kavya sat at her desk which was placed in the left corner of her room facing north, just next to a window. A full-size *khus* cooler was placed at the other end of the room forcefully pushing out the heavy hot air and replacing it with the cool, pleasant, dewy petrichor of a post-rainy afternoon.

Kavya, who was by now exhausted with her assignment, rested her face on the table and gazed dreamily through the window. She saw a sparrow sitting on the window sill. It hopped back and forth and came closer to a crack in the ledge which was filled with rain water. The bird pushed her face into the water thirstily, drank some, and with her beak she groomed herself, shaking out her feathers, fluffing her body up and then when she felt refreshed, she flew back to the tree whence she came.

Kavya noticed that as long as humans do not interfere with these tiny creatures, their mere presence infuses energy in the environment and brings so much positivity to life.

She wondered how her friend the macaw parrot was faring in its cramped cage, her stony eyes, and stationary feet.

Did it like it in there? She could feel its pain and the reason behind her agitation.

15. Mt Halton School

Unlike other classrooms in the school, Kavya's class was comparatively spacious.

Mt Halton School was the most premium educational institution in the state due to its teaching methodology.

Ms Rao entered the classroom in a neatly pleated saree and a Dutch red rose tucked in her bun. As her class was post-recess, the entire classroom was smelling of pickles, spices, and parathas. She ordered them to immediately open the windows and said with an air of annoyance, 'Why don't you guys eat lunch outside? You must get some fresh air. You will all turn into couch potatoes!'

Swaraj, a short, fair-complexioned boy raised his hand, saying, 'Ma'am, I always go out for lunch.' This was immediately echoed by a few random voices, 'Me too, ma'am.'

'Okay, okay, now, settle down. Where were we...?'

'Ma'am, The Ecosystem, page 120,' called out a helpful voice.

'Oh, yes, thank you.'

Ms Rao was an amazing teacher, who paid equal attention to every child present in the class, including those who chose to hide on the last bench. She demanded eye contact and active participation and ensured that everyone was kept engaged during her class.

At the beginning of the session, she noticed that Kavya was a little preoccupied.

'Kavya, any issues, baby?' she enquired kindly.

'No, ma'am,'

'Are you alright, darling?'

'Yes, ma'am. Thank you, ma'am.'

Ms Rao continued the class energetically and enthusiastically and in between the session, she asked them to tell her the steps to create a happy ecosystem.

Most of them raised their hands vying for her attention...except a few. One of them was Kavya who was normally one of the most attentive children in the class.

'Kavya, please, stand up.'

She rose from her seat, head hanging down.

'What's the matter, Kavya? Are you not feeling well?'

'I am alright, ma'am.'

'Come here.'

Kavya closed her book by keeping a pencil in between the pages as a marker so that she could easily find the page later.

'What's the matter?' Ms. Rao asked her again.

'I'm not feeling good about it, it's wrong. It's very wrong,' said Kavya almost in tears.

'What on Earth are you talking about?'

And this time, her tone reflected that she was beginning to lose patience. Kavya mumbled something unintelligibly, keeping her back stiff and refusing to look up.

'What parrot? Speak clearly.'

'Ma'am, it is not fair that we keep any living creature in a cramped cage forever, and that too for our amusement. I am sad and upset. Sad for the poor bird.'

'Oh, dear child, come here,' she said gently. 'You mean our new macaw parrot?'

'It has not moved since yesterday.'

'Kavya, we are taking good care of the bird.'

'You know what, we don't need to. Birds are self-sufficient creatures. They can do everything on their own, we just shouldn't interfere in their lives,' Kavya said in a rush.

'Now, please sit down,' said the teacher. 'Yes, so, where were we?'

'Ma'am, ecosystem,' said Prabhas.

'An ecosystem means a particular unit of space with living organisms, their physical environment, their interdependencies and in a world where everything coexists.'

Once the teacher left, Kavya's partner, Saisha, turned towards her and asked Kavya if she was still upset.

Kavya nodded, her eyes still moist. 'You know Saisha, when I look at the bird, I always ask myself one question, "How would I feel if I had to stay in one place all day long?" It can't even spread its wings properly! Life in captivity is like a death sentence.'

The discussion about the poor bird touched the hearts of the other students as well. Slowly, they all gathered around, listening to this serious and emotional topic over other paltry issues.

'Birds are meant to fly free and be with others of their own kind in a natural environment,' said Neha sympathetically.

Imagine, what will happen if we're kept captive even for one day all alone! I was once locked in a bathroom for just an hour, I can't tell you how creepy that one hour was! I was sweating profusely and was scared to death, I can't imagine our bird living in that cramped cage,' said Karan, shrugging his shoulders.

Everyone concurred and added their own statements.

'I think we must speak to Principal Madam about this,' said Kavya

'Yes, I agree,' said Neha

'Absolutely correct,' agreed others.

'I think ma'am will surely empathise with us. After all, she is an animal lover too.'

'Let's take an appointment for tomorrow morning.'

'Perfect.'

'Let's all sign an application request stating our reason for the meeting.'

Kavya immediately tore out a sheet from her art book and wrote:

To,

The Principal

Sub: Inhumane treatment of the macaw parrot.

Dear Madam,

We would like to meet you for an urgent issue regarding the newly brought macaw. We would like to discuss the ecosystem of the school.

Thank you and regards.

Students of 6 B.

'Alright, let's sign.'

Almost all the children signed the petition happily except the few who were engrossed in discussing video games.

'Thanks, friends, I am feeling much better now,' said Kavya.

'Thank you, Kavya, for including us in such a noble cause.'

16. Kavya and the Principal

'Good morning, little ones. How are you today? Tell me, what brings you here?' enquired the principal cheerfully.

Kavya stepped forward and said, 'Ma'am, we want to discuss with you our new macaw bird.'

'Yes, I know that, I have seen your duly signed letter. Before you guys manifest any misconceptions, let me clear your doubt here.' She called out to the peon. 'So, Mr James, please tell us how we take care of the bird.'

'Ma'am, we do everything according to the guidelines provided to us. The bird's food, water, temperature – everything is maintained appropriately.'

'Thank you so much, Mr James. You can go now.'

'But, ma'am, what about its freedom? Everyone craves for that,' said Kavya in a concerned voice.

'I guess you lot are spending too much time on an irrelevant issue. Why don't you children focus on your studies? Shivam, how much have you scored in your half-yearly exams?'

'Ma'am, 54 per cent.'

'And you, Dhruv? I heard your team lost the interschool trophy.'

Dhruv hung his head in shame.

'I guess you all have more serious areas to focus on.'

This rapid-fire exchange between the principal and the students continued.

'Now, please, go. I don't want you to miss your classes.' All the children followed the principal's instructions immediately and robotically.

'Now, focus on your studies. Turn back and go straight to your class.'

'Yes, ma'am.'

And they hurried out of the rincipal's room, pushing each other in their hurry to leave.

'And one more thing,' said the Principal in a dictatorial tone. 'That is a restricted area. No trespassing is allowed. Access is only for the primary section. Strict action will be taken against anyone who disobeys.' They stopped in their tracks listening to her.

'But madam...' said Kavya in a concerned tone.

'No buts...go straight to your classroom,' she said.

Kavya came out of the principal's office confused and walked back to class. She, however, decided that she would not give up that easily. A notice pinned outside caught her attention. *"I am still a soldier, fighting with my pen and paper for peace till the day I cease." – Emmanuel Jal*

She understood then what she needed to do.

The next morning, Kavya reached school early, kept her school bag in class, and went straight to the principal's office.

'Good morning, sir,' she wished the peon. 'Is madam inside?'

'Not yet,' answered the peon in a stern voice.

'Okay, then please hand over my letter to her when she comes, thank you.'

'Madam, may I come in?' asked the peon.

'Yes, come quickly.'

'Madam, that little girl has asked me to hand this over to you.'

The principal saw the initial on the letter, made an annoyed face and threw the letter in a nearby bin

The next day, Kavya came to the office again, handed over a letter to the principal, and marched back to class.

In hopes of seeing the magic of her pen, she wrote persistently to her principal highlighting the pathetic state of the caged bird.

Weeks passed without a response but Kavya was not one to give up that easily; with every passing day, her belief became stronger, and she knew that what she was doing was right.

She promised herself that she would finish the work she had started. Someone had to speak up for these innocent creatures!

17. Unfulfilled Dreams

'Kavya!'

'Yes, Maa?'

'What are you doing?'

Kavya was sitting in her garden with a thin twig in her hand. Lost in her thoughts, she was doodling faces in the mud with big eyes, flat noses, and frizzy curly hair.

'Kavya...'

'Yes, Maa, I am listening.'

Kavya's mum could make out that something was bothering her, and she also knew that Kavya wouldn't give up on things that easily. She wanted to help her but at the same time didn't want to interfere. She wanted her to become a sensible and self-reliant person, to be able to take her own decisions.

'Come here, Kavya,' her mother said.

Kavya threw the twig back onto the fence and came forward dusting her cotton dress, which had been stitched by her mother – a white frock with pink roses embroidered on it.

She came and sat next to her mother looking very disinterested.

'I know you are upset.'

Kavya shrugged. 'No, I am fine.'

'I know you are. Listen, baby, I know what is troubling you. Sometimes, the task that we undertake is not that easy, it requires persistence, relentless hard work, and the constant reaffirmation of our inner voice that whatever we are doing is worth the effort. To keep moving ahead, you need to remove one question from your mind, "how long?". You should never be worried about how much time it will take. Let's do one thing, get your notebook.'

'Oh, Maa, not today please.'

'Kavya, for me, please.'

Once Kavya returned with a notebook, they sat under a tree, smiling and cuddling each other, leaving their inhibitions aside and giving it one more try with an open mind and warm heart.

On a white sheet of paper, they came up with a framework.

Know your goal:

Be specific.

Be realistic.

The bigger the goal, the more work it takes.

Break it down:

Stay motivated.

Recommit to your goal if you slip up.

Have a supportive friend.

Just don't give up.

'Now, the last one is the most important of all, **never give up**, come what may,' said Mrs Murthy with her eyes misting over and a lump in her throat. Kavya held her mother's hand and buried her face in her mother's lap.

'No, Maa, please, don't cry.'

Mrs Murthy wiped her tears immediately, composed herself, and said, 'I am okay.'

'What is it, Maa? Please, tell me,' pleaded Kavya.

She said nothing, got up and went to her room, sat on the edge of her four-poster bed with the pretty white curtains around it, and wept.

Kavya was very troubled as she had never seen her mother cry like this.

She had come running behind her mother holding the corner of her saree. She sat next to her mum and asked her gently, 'Please, tell me, why you are crying. Remember you said we were each other's confidantes, best buddies? Tell me, what is it?'

Mrs Murthy got up from the bed and opened her wardrobe, pulled out an old briefcase, dusted it with her hand, and placed it carefully on the corner of the bed.

With both fingers, she clicked open the case, unveiling her hidden dreams, achievements, and passions. She took out an old scrapbook and flipped open the pages filled with cuttings from newspapers in different languages.

'Is that you, Maa?'

Kavya held the scrapbook in her hand to have a closer look; it was a young Sudha (now Mrs Murthy) topper of her school, state rank holder, and the one who had so many accolades. She flipped through all the certifications as

Kavya shook her head in disbelief, completely flabbergasted.

'Maa, you never told me about this.'

'Well, it is a buried dream now. But I don't want you to give up on anything the way I did.'

'But, Maa, you were a fantastic student.'

'Yes, I was.'

She flipped through all the certifications and then finally came across the photograph of a young lady.

'Who is she, Maa?' enquired Kavya in a voice full of excitement.

A smile surfaced on Mrs Murthy's face.

The transition from Sudha to Mrs Murthy had not been easy for her, her identity had changed, and there were a new set of expectations and a whole lot of responsibilities. Amidst all this, the young Sudha had almost faded away.

18. Sudha

Sudha was born in a small town in southern India and spent her childhood in a joint family. Living under the same roof with four siblings and six cousins ensured that there was no necessity of making friends outside of the home. And eventually, accounting for all her years in an all-girls school from kindergarten to intermediate, she managed to befriend Chandralekha, the only daughter of a doctor couple. Chandralekha was a confident child, with a fair complexion, and was of above-average height.

Together, they shared dreams that would take them on career paths that would allow them to fly high without any boundaries. They never missed a chance to spot a fighter jet in the sky, and as their town was a base camp for training pilots, there were plenty of them flying around. Their bond was stronger than that of siblings as they shared a common passion.

Sudha was raised in a family where daughters were born with extra responsibilities. They had to master not only culinary skills but also be academically gifted as only girls who obtained a first rank were considered worthy enough to marry a boy with a government job.

Sudha, however, was different. She was determined about what she wanted to achieve in life. Sorted and composed she worked hard day and night to achieve her dream to fly.

Chandralekha was a true friend and Sudha had come to rely on her a lot. She would encourage Sudha to stay focused, help her fix her priorities, and boost her confidence whenever she was down. But deep down, Sudha knew that her appa would never approve of her dream of being a pilot.

'Why do you need to inform them? Just focus on your written test,' that's what Chandralekha had told her before the exam. And so, Sudha planned to take her written exam. It was raining very heavily that day, and Sudha didn't know what excuse she could give to venture out in such bad weather. She thought to herself, *it looks as if the gods are not on my side*. She prayed for a miracle to happen and the doorbell rang.

It was Chandralekha.

'Oh, Chandra, how are you dear? Come inside,' said Sudha's mother. 'Sudha is upstairs. Come, I will make some pakoras for you.'

'Yes, Aunty,' saying this, Chandra ran upstairs to see Sudha.

'Here is your admission card and your passport-size photograph. Now, rush! We are already late.'

'But, Chandra,' said Sudha, 'what will I tell them?'

'Sudha, you just come, I will handle this.' She patted her on the shoulder and gave her a reassuring smile.

'Let's go, we have been waiting for this!'

They came down in a rush while Sudha's mum was still preparing pakoras in the kitchen.

'Aunty, it's my mum's birthday and we are planning a surprise party for her. Can I please take Sudha with me? We will be back by the afternoon. Please, please, aunty?' begged Chandra, and of course, Sudha's mum had to relent.

'Chandra you saved me today,' said Sudha.

'Yes, thanks for the vote of confidence but right now we don't have time for sweet talk.'

The examination was held in an old government school building. The walls weren't plastered, and the faded remnants of paint were peeling off with caricatures of some cartoon characters barely visible on the lower half of the walls. The lady invigilators were wearing sarees and standing at the entrance of the examination halls. The men were busy rushing in and out and trying to coordinate the swarm of students gushing in. Everyone looked tensed and rushed.

Sudha and Chandralekha checked their roll numbers and asked one of the lady teachers to guide them further.

'Show me your hall ticket,' she asked, fixing her eyeglasses. 'Oh, you go up, then take the first room on the left, and you have to go to hall number three on the ground floor.'

'Thank you, ma'am,' saying this, they rushed to their respective rooms. Once settled in her seat, Sudha took a deep breath, closed her eyes, and held a small locket that she was wearing around her neck. It was a miniature of Lord Balaji. She grasped it firmly and kissed the pendant for luck. Sudha's entire family were ardent followers of Lord Balaji. After a brief prayer, she opened her eyes and glanced at her exam paper. For the next two hours, it was just her ambition that mattered and nothing else.

Sudha was happy with the way she did in the exam and was confident that she would score well. Days passed by, and finally, the day of judgement had come.

Chandra called Sudha that morning. 'Are you coming with me? The results are out.'

'Yes, I can't miss this.'

'Maa, I will be back in an hour,' said Sudha.

'Arey, Sudha, where are you going? Your appa just called. Your aunty is coming from Bangalore. Stay at home, your appa won't like it if you're away.'

'But, Maa, I will be back in an hour.'

Before she could say another word, her father came in from outside and said in an authoritative tone, 'Stay at home, Sudha, your aunty can come anytime now. Go and help your mother in the kitchen, prepare some sweets.'

Sudha glanced at her friend, and with a calming look, Chandra nodded.

She whispered, 'Don't worry. I have a feeling that we will both be flying soon,' and she made the motion of a flying plane with her hand.

Sudha smiled and hugged her, 'Come straight back here,' said Sudha in an excited voice.

'I will,' said Chandra and they hugged each other.

Sudha stepped back with butterflies in her stomach, not knowing how to let her mother know how special this day was for her. She went to the kitchen and hugged her mother.

Sudha's mum kissed her on the forehead and said, 'I am so happy for you.'

Taken aback by this response Sudha was bewildered but kissed her back.

'Maa, what are you doing so early in the kitchen? So much preparation, what's special today?' saying this, she sat on the kitchen counter and took a bite from the plate of freshly fried *vadas*. 'Hmmm, yummy, Maa.'

Her mother smiled and patted her cheeks, a special mum-and-daughter moment was interrupted by Sudha's father.

He cleared his throat to announce his arrival. Sudha jumped off the counter and stood at attention.

'How are the arrangements going?' enquired her father.

'All going well.'

'Let me know right away in case you need something from the market, I don't want any last-minute rush,' saying this, he ducked his head slightly and stepped out.

'One more thing,' said Sudha's father, turning back, 'Ask Sudha to make one special dish.'

'Sudha has been helping me all morning. You don't worry.'

Sudha's father proceeded with a nod.

'Maa, what is happening? Why is Appa looking so serious?'

Sudha's mother smiled and held her hand, 'It's a special day today. Your aunty is coming.'

'Ya, I know, she comes every weekend. What's new about that?'

'Oh, please, don't ask questions now. You go and take a bath and wear that yellow saree, that silk one.'

'Maa, will you please tell me what is happening here?'

'Your aunty is bringing a match for you, they are coming to see you today. The boy is really nice, he works with a big multinational company. Earlier, your father was a bit sceptical, you know him, na? He is only convinced by a government job, but after meeting his family, he is quite happy. So, we have invited them for lunch.'

'Maa, how can you do this without even taking my consent?'

'Sudha, I know what you are feeling now, that your parents are very pushy. You may even feel that we are your enemies at this moment but once you are settled and will look back after a few years, you will be really happy about this decision. And when you would compare yourself and your status with your peers, I am sure you won't regret your decision.'

'And we are very proud to have a daughter like you,' said her father in a heavy and emotional tone as he joined them quietly.

Startled by his presence, Sudha hugged him tightly and wept profusely. Sudha's father kept his hand on her head, and said, 'You are the best daughter one could have, I am proud to be your father, Sudha, don't let us down ever.'

He urged her mother to take Sudha to her room and get her ready.

'We can expect them anytime now.'

'Yes, we are almost ready,' said her mother, wiping her tears.

Sudha went to her room with her mother in a state of utter confusion. She didn't know where to start, or what to tell her!

'Maa, I want to study further, I have not told you, but I have been preparing for my further studies and I lied to you. I didn't go for Chandra's mother's birthday, it was my written exam for pilot training that day.'

Sudha's mother held her by her arm pulled her roughly into the room and closed the door.

'Sudha, don't you dare say this in front of your father or he will be furious that you are hiding things.'

'Maa, you need to listen to me, it's my life and I'm not a child anymore, you can't just dictate things to me anymore,' Sudha remonstrated.

Sudha's mum looked at her with red and tearful eyes. With tears rolling down her cheeks, she quickly wiped her face and burst out emotionally, 'Now I have understood why everyone was of the opinion to not let their daughters study further. It's our fault that we sent you to the big convent school. What are the results now? You are using your education against your parents! The boy's family will be here any moment. If they get to know that the girl has refused the proposal, it will be an unbearable shame for the family. Your father will never accept this, you want to see your father hang his head in shame!'

'You can see all this, I cannot, not as long as I am alive!' So saying, she ran down to the kitchen, took a huge knife in her hand, and tried to slit her wrist.

Sudha shouted, 'No Maa, please stop, just stop there, Maa.'

'No, Sudha, you have to promise that you will not bring shame on the family.'

'Maa, please stop!' Sudha held her mother's hand firmly and with a little struggle she was able to knock the knife out of her hand.

Blood oozed from her mother's hands where she had cut herself slightly.

'Maa, no, you don't have to do this. I am your daughter and will never let you down,' cried Sudha. Sudha hugged her mother and cried inconsolably.

Sudha's father shouted out to them from the front, 'Are you coming? They are here!'

Sudha's mum immediately wiped her tears and rushed downstairs adjusting her gajra and Kanjeevaram saree.

Sudha stood still, emotionally drained as she opened her drawer and held her ID card in her hand. She stared at her small passport-size photograph. Even though it was only a small photo, her eyes were shining so passionately in that picture. What a determined and confident smile, she whispered to herself. Sudha touched her roll number on the left side of the admit card. Suddenly, there was a knock on the door.

'Sudha Didi!' Little Kusum, the neighbour's daughter, entered the room wearing an orange choli and *ghagra*. She came up close and said, 'Didi's boy is really handsome, you are so lucky, I am so excited.' She pulled Sudha's hand and handed her a set of clothes saying, 'Amma sent this for you, please change and get ready fast.'

Tears rolled down her cheeks. Her kajal was smudged. Sudha tore her admit card into shreds and sobbed.

The courtyard was filled with guests, people laughing and discussing the next steps. 'Taste the laddoos,' said Sudha's mother with a beaming smile.

Sudha slowly stepped down the stairs, wearing a bright yellow saree with red golden zari work, her hair fixed in a waist-length plait. There was an amazing fragrance coming from the jasmine *gajra* entwined in her hair.

'This is my daughter, she has just completed her high school.'

Sudha thought to herself, *I could have been better introduced had I been given a chance to prove myself.*

'She is beautiful,' uttered the boy's mother.

'Does she cook?'

'Oh, yes, taste this, Sudha makes lovely modak.'

Sudha made eye contact with her mother but she quickly looked away.

That same afternoon, her fate was sealed. Her life seemed meaningless all of a sudden.

It was so sudden for Sudha that she could not quite comprehend what had just happened; she couldn't even cry properly. With a heavy heart and a lump in her throat, she went back to her room.

As she was climbing the stairs, Chandra lunged and hugged her from behind talking excitedly and incessantly. 'I cannot believe this, Sudha! We did it! Both of us!'

She shook her briskly to awaken her from her reverie. 'Are you listening, Sudha?'

And then she saw Sudha's face as a flood of tears came from her eyes.

'Hey, Sudha, what happened?'

Sudha hugged her friend, her only confidante, and sobbed inconsolably.

Chandra held her tight, wiped her tears, and took her back to her room, hoping she would open up in private.

'It's over, Chandra, I told you they would never agree.'

'No, Sudha, don't say this. You and only you can take that call. Stand up for yourself Sudha, it's your life, and you have to build it.'

Sudha shook her head and wiped her tears. With a hoarse voice, she said, 'I think I'm really lucky, the boy is really good, an only son with a good job in a multinational company. I think it's time for me to settle down,' and a fake smile surfaced on her face.

'No, Sudha, I won't let you do this. Never. You come with me right now,' and Chandra dragged her out of her room holding her hand.

'No, Chandra, please stop.'

'Sudha, you just need to speak for yourself, please don't make your life a joke. You worked hard like an idiot, for what? Just to settle for this in your life? They don't even know what a star you are!' Chandra was speaking fast, her words tripping over each other, a reflection of her frustration and helplessness.

'Chandra, I request you to leave.'

'But, Sudha, this is not correct.'

'I said leave, Chandra, just leave.' Sudha hid her face from her friend as she did not want her to see the anguish in her eyes.

'Alright, I am leaving. But one thing is for sure, we are no longer friends from today. I don't know any Sudha.' She was furious and hurt and repeated, 'I don't know any Sudha,' saying this, she tore the scorecard into pieces and left Sudha forever.

19. Crazy Bunch

Kavya sat at her desk with Chandra's photo in her hand. It was very inspiring for Kavya to personally see a woman in an officer's uniform. She felt like saluting the photograph but kept her feelings in check for a day when she could meet her in person. She pinned the photo on her soft board above her study desk.

Kavya was a very organised child. From neatly stacked stationery to books placed in the subject order, she kept it all spick and span. Her pin board was meticulously arranged with her school timetable and a few recently made sketches. Medals were hung up with red and blue ribbons to the right side of the board, her to-do list was highlighted with a fluorescent marker, important news cuttings were pinned neatly one below the other and at the top of this list was the picture of the macaw. She held the photo in her hand and studied the colourful plumage of its wing, *what a beautiful creation of nature! How fortunate it would be to see it flying high in the sky, flapping its wings carefreely and reflecting the rainbow colours of the sun!*

She took a deep breath, opened her diary and picked up her blue ink fountain pen. In the top margin, she made a Swastik sign, (her good-luck ritual which she had picked up from her mother).

Below that, she wrote in capital letters.

MISSION MACAW

Objective:

Planning:

She reminded herself that since she had taken on the responsibility of saving the bird, the onus was on her to take it to the finish line!

She was 100 per cent convinced about her decision but figuring out a solution was like walking a maze! In a state of utter confusion, she lay back in her recliner, closed her eyes, and exhaled deeply.

Ting tong!

Her reverie was broken by the sudden tintinnabulation of the doorbell. She twisted her head and glanced out of her room.

Mrs Murthy came out of the kitchen, wiping her face with the corner of her pallu.

'Namaste, aunty!' Kavya's group of friends greeted in unison.

'Oh, hello, children! Please, come in.'

'Thank you, aunty,' said Saisha in her chirpy voice.

Kavya leaned back in disbelief. 'Hey!' she shouted. 'What are you guys doing here?'

She pushed herself out of the chair and rushed towards the living room. She excitedly hugged Saisha and high-fived her other classmates.

'Kavya, take them to your room, I will bring in some snacks for you,' said Mrs Murthy.

'Wow, that's amazing décor, Kavya. I presumed a girl's room would be a miniature dollhouse with pink walls and a princess bed. The rugged look of your room impresses me, especially these miniature aircraft models,' said Karan.

Kavya cleared her throat and spoke with a great sense of pride, 'Well, these are handcrafted DIY fighter jet models. My mum is an incredible craftsman.'

'Awesome, Kavya, you never mentioned this before.'

'Yes, I never thought it would catch your eye!'

'No, seriously, Kavya, I love the rough textured wall and your bunk bed reflects you have real rock star taste.'

'Oh, yes, what a nicely organised room!' Saisha piped in cheerfully.

'I am so happy that you are all here,' Kavya smiled back. 'You don't know how badly I needed you.'

'We know,' said Karan. 'We all know, and honestly speaking, we desperately wanted to see you too. We want to join you in your mission. Let's make it big this time,' he finished in a rush.

'So, what's the plan?' asked Neha, pushing her spectacles up her nose. Neha was a junior volunteer member with PETA.

Karan hopped onto the top of the bunk bed while Saisha and Neha made themselves comfortable on the lower bed. Kavya sat at her desk and cleared her throat. 'Okay, so without wasting any time, let me give you an update on the information I got from the web.'

'Go ahead,' said Saisha.

She opened the folder named Macaw.

'See here, I have gathered some information about the Wildlife Protection Act,' she turned her screen so that everyone could see.

- The rainforests are being cut down at an alarming rate, which is a serious threat to the future survival of all macaw species.
- More than five species of macaw are already extinct.
- The illegal wildlife trade is the third-largest black-market industry in the world.
- Poachers usually target nestlings during the breeding season as eggs can be less cumbersome to transport than live birds.
- The illegal bird trade poses an immediate threat to the species' survival.
- Poaching is associated with a very high mortality rate. It is estimated that approximately 75% of the birds taken from the wild die in transit.

'You know what, guys? I think it is important to bring these heart-wrenching facts in front of everyone,' Karan suggested.

'Yes, I know! But how?' said Kavya.

'Social media,' said Karan.

Everyone rolled their eyes sarcastically at him.

'At least give me a chance to explain,' said Karan.

'Proceed,' chorused the girls.

'Okay, so listen. We are living in an electronic age where the power of social media is immense, and one can connect, share and exchange information with anyone on Earth, with millions of people in a split second.'

Their eye rolls now changed to a serious nod. 'I think Karan is absolutely correct. Social media is a powerful tool,' said Neha.

'Yes, this could be a powerful instigator for positive social change. Transforming opinions...' Karan trailed off.

'Yeah, so actually, social media is not just to post fancy pictures to show off your puppy's birthday bash; it can be used for much more,' said Neha.

'Much more like what?' asked Saisha.

'We've all come across Facebook fundraisers for bigger causes like the Australian bushfire or the Black Lives Matter movement. These movements were extremely impactful, originating from one pole to reaching the other end of the world in fractions of seconds,' explained Neha.

'Yeah, exactly how a sensitive tweet can bring down oil prices or can shake up the stock market. You know, a small act of Cristiano Ronaldo removing two Coca-Cola bottles from his interview table and urging people to drink water instead cost Coca-Cola 4 billion dollars from their market share; all because it was caught on international TV! Such a strong and impressive ripple reaction can only happen through social media,' Karan added.

'That's a very nice idea, I think this is a good platform to bring forth the plight and suffering of these remarkable creatures,' said Kavya.

'Brilliant, well done, Karan!' said Neha.

Karan bowed low and smiled in acknowledgement.

'The only way to do big things is to stop thinking and start acting,' said Neha with a gleaming smile on her face. 'What's a better day than Sunday to start something special like this?'

They all excitedly high-fived in agreement.

'So, let's get started. Hey, wait, we might need to get our parents' preapproval, or at least from one of our parents,' Neha pointed out.

'Oh, yes, Neha is right, since we all are under 13, we are not yet at the legally permissible age to have independent social media accounts,' Kavya reminded them.

'But who is going to support us now?'

'Oh, kids, not that close to the screen please,' exclaimed Kavya's mother as she entered the room with a tray of mixed pakoras and *dal wadi* in her hands.

As soon as she kept the tray down, Karan lunged forward and picked one.

'Be careful...' she warned him but before she could finish her sentence, Karan gobbled the pakora.

'Ohh, it's so hot!' Karan fanned his mouth with his hand, exhaling warm air and hopping on one foot trying to keep the hot pakora from burning his mouth.

'That's why I was telling you to be careful, they're piping hot!'

'But really yummy,' he said, reaching for another. The girls burst out laughing at his crazy antics.

'Maa, listen.'

'What, another kitchen request?'

'No, Maa, do you think we are foodies?'

'Are you asking me or telling me, lady?'

'Maa, tell me one thing – do you have a Facebook account?'

'Yes,' said Kavya's mom.

'Okay, that's cool, na?'

'What's so cool about it?'

'I mean it's like you can connect with people all around the world. You can share your ideas and your views. There are so many things we can do digitally.'

'Come to the point, young lady,' Mrs Murthy said impatiently.

'Aunty, actually we want to create a social media handle to give voice to our cause as we feel this is one of the most effective ways to connect with a large audience simultaneously,' explained Neha.

'Hmm, that sounds really great, but how are you going to do that?'

'Aunty, we want to start a movement.'

'A movement. Okay, that's nice,' she agreed.

'We're gonna call it, "It's our Planet Too",' said Neha. 'We want to create a page for this where we can educate people about the harsh realities of bird trafficking, how badly they are being treated by being kept in those cramped cages, and all other abuses they have to undergo.'

'That's a great idea,' said Mrs Murthy. 'Social media is one of the biggest influencers nowadays. I'm there. Let me know when and how I can be of any help.'

'Thank you so much, Aunty,' they all responded in relieved and cheerful voices.

'Guys! Thank you so much for dropping by. I feel so much better now,' said Kavya.

'No, Kavya, thanks to you, at least we have got something positive to do during this summer break, rather than eating calorie bombs made by my granny.'

'Yeah, I annoyed my father to get me a geared bicycle, but with this new project, I know he too can take a sigh of relief,' said Karan.

The innocent little children, laughing, chatting, and eating pakoras were not aware that they were initiating a big move. A kind of butterfly effect was at play where the smallest change could result in vastly different outcomes and would help in changing something nasty into something remarkable. With fire in them, they spoke passionately and confidently with their eyes rolling from left to right, now focused on one goal.

Yes, we will do it.

20. Changemaker

Living in a digital era where technology is at our beck and call, finding their way on social media may be challenging for others. But for the youngsters of today, it is a breeze. For these power-packed kids, a digital platform is an easier option compared to the conventional methods of library research. Within no time at all, they had created an engaging home page and put it online. They gave the page an alluring name – "Changemaker". A description of their movement 'It's Our Planet Too' was mentioned and at the end, a beautiful picture of the macaw was added to the page. Within a few seconds of the page going live, it showed one "like".

'Hey, look at that!' Karan screamed excitedly. 'People are liking our page. Isn't that awesome?'

'Commendable effort, children! I'm really happy to see such impressive work.' Kavya's mum stood there with her hands folded and a smile on her face.

'Really, Sudha Aunty? You think so?'

'Certainly,' she said, 'I am sure your efforts will bring results soon.'

The twinkle in their eyes reflected the glow of passion and commitment on their faces.

It was important to keep the page updated with fresh news every week. Slowly, the circle of volunteers increased, everyone was keen and wanted to contribute. The children stayed back for after-school meetings and discussions voluntarily without displaying a hint of tiredness on their faces.

The entire school had begun to show interest and as the students from the intermediate sections joined the league, there was a wave of excitement. Some contributed through incisive advice while others sponsored Parle-G biscuits and cold water as refreshments.

The overall spirit was high, and the goal was clear. Within a few days, the Facebook page was a popular site for all children; it was trending, and people were tweeting about it. They viewed it, commented, and of course, liked the page.

The power of the internet and social media was making waves, and pretty soon, it had become a social movement.

The newly appointed team of volunteers was so engrossed in their work that they literally missed the upcoming Onam festival. The school was about to close, which meant it would be tough for them to meet at school.

They chalked out a plan for after-school meetings. Careful planning was needed now as the strength of the group had increased manifold. A group of higher-grade students walked up and greeted them.

'Hey, you guys are doing a good job,' said Naira who was in the 12th standard, the senior most grade in their school. As a mark of respect, they all rose to make way for the seniors. They were all sitting under the shade of the big mango tree – and though it never bore any fruit, the heavy foliage of the leafy branches was enough to give shelter to more than a dozen children. The only drawback of sitting under the tree was that it was home to all kinds of creepy crawlies from ants to spiders and thousands of birds that were perched on the thick and dense branches. So, every now and then one of them would be blessed by the birds!

Naira continued with her air of sophistication and confidence, 'So, we have been reading all your posts, and let me tell you that it's awesome, guys!'

'Thank you,' said Saisha in her charming voice.

'Great till now, but what are you guys planning next?' enquired Naira.

'Things were smooth till here but since school is closing, we are a little concerned about offline after-school meetings,' said Kavya.

'Yes, it will be tough to coordinate without meet-ups.'

'Yeah, we will need to brainstorm and plan to keep up the momentum.'

'But without these meetings, we will miss big time,' said Karan.

'Hmm, I know what you will miss,' said Neha and snatched a pack of cream biscuits from his hand.

'Alright, now listen, if you guys are seriously looking for a meeting place, I mean a serious meeting, then I can definitely help,' said Naira. 'You can try Wisdom Library. You can hold your meeting there till the time school reopens. It is just a few metres away from our school.'

'No no no, we can't go to Wisdom Library, Mrs Joseph is very grumpy,' objected Karan.

'Oh, by the way, she happens to be my mother,' said Naira glaring at him and arching her eyebrow.

'Oh, is that so? I think I'm confused, I don't think I've ever been to Wisdom Library,' said Karan, scratching his head and making a quick recovery.

'Oh, please ignore what he said, I apologise on his behalf,' jumped in Kavya.

'Oh, that's absolutely fine. So, let's freeze the plan, 9 to 12 noon.'

'Sounds terrific,' shouted Neha in excitement.

'Great, then, see you tomorrow!'

'And one more thing – a few of our seniors are working with Animal Rehab Centre. I think we should invite them too,' added Naira.

'Oh, that's an awesome idea.'

'Kavya, I think you should prepare a presentation that will look a bit more organised and show your seriousness and commitment to the cause,' suggested Naira.

'If that's the case, we will definitely present.'

'Best of luck, guys!' said Naira. 'And you, little brat, behave!'

21. Presentation Day

Five Animal Rehab Centre representatives were already seated in the comfortable leather chairs by the time Kavya and her team reached the reading room of the library.

Karan peeped into the reading room, and the cold breeze of the air conditioning hit his nose. He quickly checked out the room and rushed towards his friends saying it looked like an interview panel.

'It's okay, Karan, there's nothing to worry about,' Kavya reassured him.

'Are you nervous?' teased Neha.

'Oh, nervous for what?'

Kavya knocked on the door and walked in, politely wishing them all a good morning.

'Oh, please, come in.'

Kavya signalled her team to step inside. They opened the door and marched in – confident of their moves with passion in their eyes. They sat across from the panel and Kavya was requested to present.

Kavya stood up, opened her PowerPoint presentation, and spoke with utmost confidence. Seeing her clarity of thought and passion about the cause, Mrs Chitra Banerjee, the area manager of the state, applauded their effort and said that we will officially support the cause, and whatever they required to bring about this change, they would do together. They came out of the room grinning like Cheshire cats!

Naira came rushing out of the room, and said in a cheerful voice, 'Congratulations, guys, you did it, they loved your work. How nicely you presented, Kavya. Awesome job!'

'Oh, thank you. But one thing is for sure, it wouldn't have been possible without your help.' Kavya smiled gratefully.

22. Jonah

The shallow unintentional tremor caused by the rag-tag group of schoolchildren was no longer restricted to the state and national borders. Thanks to social media, the effect of their work had snowballed into a revolutionary movement and was now being talked about even in the most remote corners of the Earth.

The vibrations were felt all the way in Honduras, an exotic coastal country in Central America, bounded by the Caribbean Sea. The Scarlet Macaw is their national bird and adds to the main attraction of the country, which is an abundance of wildlife. People travel from across the world to this wonderland to witness the Scarlet Macaw easily recognisable by its bright red, blue, and yellow plumage. The stunning and picturesque landscape, rugged mountains, and deep valleys are merely the icing on the cake when it comes to describing this country.

But as we mentioned earlier, "its beauty has become its bane". The macaw's magnificent looks are instrumental to its decreasing population. In recent years, their population has been decimated by the illegal wildlife trade. Poachers snatch eggs and chicks from wild nests, clip their wings, and smuggle birds not only within Honduras but also to other parts of the world.

A young Spanish girl, Jonah lived with her father in San Pedro, the second largest city in Honduras, and had grown up hearing stories of how activists had been killed while protecting their river forests and land.

Mr Bosaro, Jonah's father, was a well-recognised environmental activist who had dedicated his life to the conservation of the forests and the wildlife of Honduras. On the one hand, the country is extremely rich in natural resources but on the other, it is one of the poorest countries in Latin America.

Mr Bosaro was the foster father of Jonah. Her biological parents had died during one of the deadliest natural disasters that had devasted Central America during the summer of 1998 – Hurricane Mitch.

Mr M Jollies and his wife Ritz had succumbed to their injuries in the aftermath of the hurricane, and since then, little Joanna had been living with her uncle – Mr Bosaro. They shared a beautiful bond and seeing them together, no one would even think that Mr Bosaro was not her biological father. A picture-perfect family, where a sweet daughter and loving father do things together –– be it combing Jonah's tangled curly hair, a task which she would make extra difficult by running through the house, just out of his reach, and he would be following with a hairbrush in his hands; or standing on the step stool to reach the height of the mirror, where she could see her reflection and make funny faces while brushing her teeth while following her dad's instructions. Most mornings when the weather was good, Jonah would enjoy her dad's workout sessions, sitting on his back while he did push-ups, or sometimes sitting on a tree branch, and helping him count his reps. Their father-daughter bond was exceptional and enviable.

Jonah had now grown into a beautiful girl with a sweet smile and a God-gifted charm. The transition from a vulnerable toddler to a confident and bold girl was miraculous. Jonah now supported her father in his work in whichever way possible – be it organising his desk, assisting him with research work, or looking after the funding of his current projects like painting competitions, poster making, road shows, and many more activities that she was actively involved in.

At the same time, Jonah would also help her father in preparing meals or managing laundry. She would just wait for him to come home so that she could go on nonstop about school or plans for weekends.

Weekends usually started with a football match stretching into a lazy afternoon sitting by the lake with their fishing rods, or sometimes an exciting ride out to sea to watch the dolphins. And in the evening, they would envisage a prosperous future for the people of Honduras.

The declining number of scarlet macaws was now a major concern for Jonah. The young conservationist had not left any stone unturned in her efforts to protect the existence of the national bird. One sunny day, when Jonah was doing her research work, she came across a social media movement that was doing its rounds on the internet. A bunch of young school children from Asia, who called themselves the Changemaker were the driving force behind the movement "It's Our Planet Too".

Hmm...looks interesting, she thought and clicked the page. There were interesting clips of rescued birds, tagged stories, 1000s of followers, and a million likes. The social media page was an amalgamation of people from different time zones and different geographies, all voicing their opinion about the heartless treatment meted out to these helpless creatures.

'Dad, are you there?' she shouted from her desk. 'Check this out! Dad...Dad...Come here! Like right now!' she urged him impatiently.

Mr Bosaro turned in his swivel chair and wheeled it towards Jonah.

'What is it, my little baby?'

Jonah was very excited now and had opened the page.

'Check this out, these kids from India are doing a crazy job, Dad. They have a Facebook page with millions of followers.'

'And what is all the noise about?' asked Mr Bosaro, trying to get an understanding of it.

'So, there are a few Asian kids from India who have taken the internet by storm. Yeah, like check out their movement to save macaws. There is a scarlet macaw caged in their school. How can people keep these birds in a cage...' she trailed off, shaking her head in disbelief.

'Yeah...I mean, as per the law of the land, it is criminal to cage a native bird but definitely allowed for exotic species. Birds are birds, how can we be inhuman to one species and protective towards the other.'

'Absolutely...' agreed her father.

'So, they are raising their voice against the system. And to my utter surprise, this has attracted the attention of a lot of people from different regions...that's crazy, look at this, there are road shows, seminars, etc.'

'They want this macaw to be sent back to its natural habitat, how nice, right, Dad?'

After a moment's thought, Jonah said, 'Hey, Dad, I want you to help them.'

'Oh, Jonah. That's, that's...' he blustered.

'Tough. I know, Dad, but I so wanna help these kids,' said Jonah. 'Please, Dad,' she pleaded, wrapping her arms around him.

'Hmmm, alright, let me see what we can do for them.'

The next morning, there was a tweet from Mr Bosaro appreciating the team and the work they had been doing, promising them total support from his side. That single tweet by Mr Bosaro, a renowned conservationist and activist, resulted in a Twitter storm that was picked by mainstream media in a jiffy.

The massive outpouring of support from national and international followers was a huge motivator for the children. There were tweets supporting the movement, and people writing about their disappointments with the inhuman treatment of animals and birds.

There were stories about rescue missions being tagged on the page. Their efforts were being recognised.

23. Silver Lining

The next morning, Neha called. 'Hey, Kavya, have you checked your email?'

'What! Neha, it's 6 o'clock, I generally sleep till 7 and you know that.'

'You won't be able to if I tell you what bombed our mailbox.'

'Hey, come straight to the point, what is it?' enquired Kavya with a hint of irritation in her voice.

'Kavya, we've received a mail from the Macaw Recovery, Rehab & Release Centre from Central America!'

'What are you saying?'

'And...'

'What and...'

'They are ready to fly back our dear macaw!'

'Oh, my God...I can't believe this!'

'Yes, it's unbelievable. Finally, after months of waiting our efforts have paid off. And check out the last line of the mail yourself.'

'Oh...what is it...oh, my god!'

'They have invited us to visit Honduras!'

For a moment, Kavya forgot to breathe. She couldn't believe what she had just read.

Dear Ms Kavya,

We would like to congratulate you for your commendable efforts.

It feels so good to see young kids like you doing a selfless job.

We take pleasure in informing you that the Government of Honduras would like to bring back its national treasure – our beloved Scarlet Macaw.

Also, we would like to have your gracious presence for our annual cultural meet. We are excited to announce that your team has been awarded the title of "Nature Saviour".

Please sign the consent form attached to the mail and send it back ASAP

Thank you.

Marie Chappel

'Is this a dream? Neha, I can't trust my eyes...pinch me!' said Kavya.

'Kavya, I can't pinch you, I can't just pop out of the phone.'

24. Maiden Flight to Honduras

Kavya, Neha, Saisha, and Karan, were waiting at the airport with their boarding passes.

'I have never been on such a long flight,' muttered Karan. 'I mean it's so thrilling to imagine that you get to spend an entire day in the sky. Oh, I'm super excited. I wish I could open the window and feel the clouds with my hand.'

At this, all three girls turned to look at him and shook their heads in disbelief.

'Oh, come on, I said I wish, I'm not actually going to open the window,' said Karan, getting annoyed.

Kavya was always interested in her surroundings; she looked around the airport to see what unique things would catch her eye.

Travel cases were so stylish and funky these days. It was almost as if people were trying to match their personalities with their hand luggage. An elderly couple of jet setters with Starbucks coffee in their hands were sitting on the corner bench. They had two very stylish-looking bags which were lightweight with smooth wheels and a beige exterior.

On the other side, a lady was working on a flat-screen laptop, wearing black formal trousers and coffee-coloured heels. Her stylish hand luggage was from a premium travel luggage company, and the handmade logo was embossed on it.

There was a Korean family crossing gate number 4 and they had a luggage chair! What a great invention that allowed them to drag their child and their luggage through the airport with one hand still free – much needed for all mothers.

Finally, there was a boarding announcement for their plane. They took a deep breath and hurried through the gate, and with VIP passes in their hands, they were escorted through on priority.

'Quicker and crowd-free, that's what I cherish,' exclaimed Karan.

They quickly settled down. All four had made their own arrangements to keep boredom at bay for the next 30 hours of the journey with the help of puzzles, games, sketchbooks, earphones, books, etc. Kavya was curious and wanted to know more about their travel destination. So, she opened her laptop and researched Honduras, getting a brief about the political and geographical details. She explored the pristine beauty of Honduras with drowsy eyes and eventually fell asleep.

It was a dreamy afternoon – a little foggy and somewhat hazy. Sitting under a giant kapok tree was a beautiful girl clad in a cool summer dress and her golden hair cascaded down to her waist. She was playing with a colourful bird, laughing and giggling. And at last, when she looked up, it was Kavya herself. For a moment, she felt disoriented and opened her bleary eyes and looked around. She saw Neha sleeping with her mouth open and saliva drooling from the end of her mouth. It was then that Kavya realised it was all a dream.

'Wow,' she muttered to herself. She closed her eyes again to see if she could continue with her dream, but she just couldn't go back.

25. Welcome to Honduras

Covering an area of more than 15000 kilometres, the aerial view of the forest was like looking down into a massive zen garden. The entire landscape was covered with gigantic trees with leaves of mesmerising colours, sizes, and shapes. Streams of water zig-zagged through the entire land as if showering the blessings of life on the soil of Honduras. Everything that comes in touch with water automatically comes back to life – a Midas touch.

Amidst this nature's wonderland, there was a colonial-style government mansion.

The border fence around it was electrified with a couple of gunmen standing guard to boot, just to ensure that they did not rely completely on machines. Their bus arrived at the main gate of the bungalow and a tall girl with curly golden hair was smiling at them at the entrance, waving out to them joyously.

'Oh, look, that's Jonah!' said Kavya, and they waved cheerfully back to her.

The bus came to a halt with a screeching sound. They stepped out of the bus and were welcomed by the cultural team with garlands of fresh exotic flowers, and to their utter surprise, they were greeted with a *Namaste*! (A traditional Indian gesture which has different interpretations, but the most popular one being that God resides in everyone. The gesture of the palms coming together at chest level is an acknowledgement of the soul in one person by the soul in another).

'Glad to meet you all after such a long journey,' said Jonah.

'Yes, it was,' said Kavya in a composed way, trying to hide her excitement about the flying experience.

'Welcome, I will show you to your accommodation.'

It was a huge flat structure with an expansive single-storey construction. The outer facade was built with locally sourced stones giving a feel of an ultra-luxurious forest lodge. Jonah escorted them through the main corridor and as they walked through the corridor, impressive wall decor made with recycled materials caught their attention.

'This is beautiful,' expressed Kavya, touching the artefact on the wall.

'Indeed, it is,' said Jonah. 'All our sculptures are made with recycled materials. So, if you look at this one,' she said, pointing towards a colourful sculpture of horses in the wild. 'It's made up of recycled cans, no colour touch up also, this beautiful rainbow colour is all made with crushed multicoloured cans.'

As they moved ahead, they saw beautifully decorated walls with broken twigs, ceramic waste, bottle caps, unused leftover crayons, and at last the Earth monster of plastic bags. As they entered the main lobby, they saw a gigantic sculpture of a macaw with magnificent colours, made out of marble. And as the sun's rays touched the surface of the marble, they reflected the entire spectrum of the prism, illuminating the entire hall like the northern lights.

'This is so awesomely beautiful!' exclaimed the children in unison.

'Ought to be. That's why it's our national bird.'

'You guys must be worn out and so jet-lagged,' said Jonah, handing over the keys to their room. 'You need to get up early for your visit to Macaw Mountain, and trust me, you need some rest. It's going to be a physically demanding trip.'

'Well, I will take that piece of advice, I am really tired,' said Karan, and grabbed the keys to his room.

'Have a nice stay, Karen. Oh! It's Karan, but you know what, Karen sounds better,' Jonah smiled.

Karan took the keys and went straight to his room.

It's an amazing feeling that I have got my own room, even though it's just for a few days. But at least I have the bed and bathroom to myself, without having to share with anyone, thought Karan. He had been sharing a room with his elder brother, and like all big brothers, his brother was bossy at times, taking most of the bed, and using the washroom for more than the usual time. So, Karan was excited that at least for a few days, he could live his life on his own terms.

Neha, Saisha and Kavya also took their keys and bid her bye. Tired after the longest journey of their life, they slept like babies – peaceful and undisturbed.

26. Macaw Mountain

Macaw Mountain was grown out of a mission by a couple of American expatriates to care for stressed-out birds who had been mistreated as pets.

A multifaceted eco-tourism project, it was located on ten acres of forested terrain. One could be truly immersed in the richness of Honduran bird diversity while wandering about in the wonderful botanical gardens which were filled with endemic and towering hardwood trees.

Macaw Mountain provided its visitors with a personal encounter with the fascinating birds of Honduras in a natural environment. The park had a natural trail that stretched all along the canyon. The park also included an outdoor information centre where you could interact with some of the birds and take pictures. The visit was relaxing, educational, and very memorable.

Finally, they reached Macaw Mountain.

They walked through the trail and it looked as if the place belonged to them. It was all in its pristine natural form – no tree had ever been chopped down, and even when a tree had been uprooted by storms or strong winds, it still stayed horizontal. Undisturbed, gigantic mushrooms had blossomed over them.

They trekked through the park, witnessing the miracles of nature. Hot springs made the place misty and mysterious.

They eventually reached a place where the birds were seen in the wild. A giant cage was already there with all the cameramen and the entire team from the rehabilitation centre – it was a big day for everyone.

A chip was attached to the bird to keep track of its health. This was going to be a big change for the captive macaw. They thanked Kavya and the team for rescuing the helpless bird and contributing to its rehabilitation. The founder of the national park slowly opened the cages. But the miserable bird did not budge. The macaw did not budge; almost as if it had forgotten that it had wings and could fly away at will.

A volunteer stepped forward and place some kernels of corn just outside the cage. Slowly, the bird stepped forward, filled its beak with the juicy crushed corn, and flapped its wings. As the majestic creature opened its wings to its full span, one could witness a perfect embodiment of all the dominant colours of nature – a sublime wonder. The macaw flapped them again, and within no time, it took its first flight and flew up, round and round, soaring to greater heights. What a spectacular moment! All eyes were glued to the sky.

'A sign of distress,' said the health officer. 'She's flying in unusual patterns. Hey, now see, she is gliding through the air above the mountain as if she is scared to stop.'

There was a grin on everyone's face, compassion in their eyes, a sense of satisfaction from selfless service, and a feeling of giving back to nature.

Pictures were clicked as people were clapping.

Finally, the macaw came to terms with its freedom and settled down on a branch of a giant tree where other birds were also nestled harmoniously.

What a blissful sight.

Interaction with the Visionaries

I am happy you have written a book on foreign birds in India. In my office, I have 23 love birds, finches, and budgies who fly around free in the room but I have no idea where they can go since they will be killed if we leave them out. The law since 2018 is that no pet shops can sell animals or birds but not one has closed and so much smuggling of birds goes on that it is frightening to see whole countries losing their native species. These birds I have rescued are all from pavement cages and many of them turned out to be coloured munias which we released once the colour was taken off.

Maneka Sanjay Gandhi
People For Animals

Peta India

Tell us more about Peta & the work that they do?

People for the Ethical Treatment of Animals (PETA) India is a well-known animal rights group in the country that works under the simple principle that animals are not ours to eat, wear, experiment on or use for entertainment. We work hard to establish and defend the rights of animals and treat them with love and respect. We focus primarily on the areas in which the greatest numbers of animals suffer the most such as laboratories, food industry, the leather trade and in the entertainment business. For more details log onto PetaIndia.com.

What was one of your most touching bird rescue missions?

A concerned citizen reported to PETA India's emergency number that a parrot was being held against his will inside of a civilian residence for more than 5 years in Kozhikode, and our rescue team didn't waste any time in springing into action. Indian parrot species (parakeet) are protected under Schedule IV of the Wildlife protection act, 1972, and keeping them as a pet can cost you a jail term of up to 3 years and a fine up to Rs. 25,000 or both.

To liberate this innocent parrot from a solitary life behind bars where everything natural and important to him was being denied, we got in touch with the forest rangers of Thamarassery, who have the legal authority to deal with such cases. The Forest rangers team soon arrived on the scene and rescued the parrot. After a medical examination the parrot was sent to the Thamarassery Rehabilitation Centre. If he regains his ability to fly, the parrot will eventually be released back into the wild, if not, he will live a happy and healthy life at the rehabilitation centre.

Any message for the people who keep birds as pets?

Life in captivity is often a death sentence for birds who may suffer from malnutrition, an improper environment, loneliness, and the stress of confinement. Birds are meant to fly and be with others of their own kind in a natural environment. Confinement causes birds to have temper tantrums and mood swings. Birds belong in the wild, not in cages.

What's your view on legal protection given to Native birds but not to "Exotic birds",

Caging any Indian bird is illegal as they are categorized under wild animals and are thus protected by the Wildlife (Protection) Act of 1972. Not only do exotic and foreign birds fall under this category, the Wild Life (Protection) Act of 1972 provides a legal framework for the protection of different species of wild animals and plants, management of their habitats, regulation, and control of trade in wild animals, plants, and products made from them.

What would you like to say about the book," It's our planet too"

All living beings on this earth have equal rights, the right to live and the right to enjoy everything that is available on this planet. Animal have rights that must be respected just like those of humans. Your book is a great initiative that will help in creating awareness about the rights of animals and will go a long way in informing people that birds belong in the wild and not in cages.

Christopher Castle

Macaw Conservation (Costa Rica)

(www.macawconservation.org)

1. Tell us more about your organization & the work that they do.

Macaw Conservation is located on the Osa Peninsula in Costa Rica, founded in 2014, the project has done rescue and rehabilitation for the release of scarlet macaws, the project also provides sanctuary for unreleasable macaws.

2. What was one of your most touching bird rescue missions?

One very memorable rescue experience was of a 23 day old Scarlet Macaw chick who was found cold and abandoned on the forest floor by a tour guide doing a nocturnal tour in Drakes Bay at the top of the Osa Peninsula. A mystery as to how she got there, nest tree broke? Predator? Poached? the people that found her named her Milagro, or Miracle. we were contacted that morning and drove the 2hr drive to collect her. She was very weak and ill, and we treated her for the next two weeks. She then began improving and gaining good weight and started developing feathers.

Once weaned Mila then spent 18 months growing and becoming more independent in one of the rehabilitation aviaries. Till it was time for her release to join a flock of already established released macaws from previous years.

The day of her release, One of the older released macaws named Monster, (because of his size, not his personality, he's a really gentle macaw) immediately flew to Mila and protected her from the rest of the flock. From that day on they have been inseparable.

The past two seasons they have raised and fledged a clutch of two chicks each year, and are very proud parents

3. Do you get along better with humans or animals?

I get along with both Humans and Animals, but generally, Animals are easier to understand.

4. Describe a typical Working day.

A typical working day:

Feed all the sanctuary Macaws and animals

Clinic

Collect wild nuts and fruits for 2nd Feed

Cleaning, grounds, Aviaries maintenance,

2nd feed

Fieldwork

Office time

Cleaning + sanctuary dishes

5. Any message for the people who keep birds as pets?

We need to recognise Parrots and birds as sentient beings that require as much natural elements and freedoms as we humans need to live happy lives.

6. What's your view on legal protection given to Native birds but not to "Exotic birds",

I believe it's a step in the right direction, there is a need for globally recognised husbandry standards for Avicultural practices. And that there is a need for education of what different species requirements are. Aviculture has provided an important conservation tool in bringing species back from the brink of extinction, if there is wildlife, then rescue and rehabilitation centres and sanctuaries are needed also.

Exotic species should receive the same protection, but hopefully through education, people's awareness will help change this.

Thank You Priya! Please do keep in contact.

Carey Wentz
Macaw Recovery Network
www.macawrecoverynetwork.org

1. Tell us more about Macaw Recovery Network & the work that they do?

Macaw Recovery Network is a parrot conservation organization that takes a holistic approach to conservation. We protect wild parrots in their habitats, boost populations by breeding captive confiscated parrots for release, and work with local communities in Costa Rica to restore habitat and educate about these iconic birds. We have three main pillars to our conservation approach:

2. When did you realize you wanted to be a Wild Life Conservationist?

There was never a time of my life where I didn't want to work with animals. I was really inspired by Jane Goodall and how her approach to conservation changed the way biologists view wild animals. Then, when I was in college I saw footage of human and elephant conflict, where the elephants were viewed as pests and were as a result attacked when they would enter villages. This footage hurt my heart, and I felt compelled to be a voice for wild animals, who are often misunderstood by people. They can't speak for themselves, so I feel it is my responsibility to educate people for them.

3. Describe a typical Working day.

This varies depending on which site that we are working. But all days begin early, to the sounds of macaws and howler monkeys waking up in the wild around us. And they end with the sounds of those same animals going home for the night. It's a beautiful thing to work surrounded by the nature we are working hard to protect.

4. Do you get along better with humans or animals?

As an introvert, I have always gotten along better with animals. However, in order to create a better world for animals, as conservationists we must work with people. Without community involvement, conservation efforts will not have lasting impact.

5. If you have to give a piece of advice to people across the world what would that be?

In order for our planet to recover and thrive, we must approach every conservation issue with compassion; to each other, to wildlife, and to our planet.

6. What are your views about the book "It's our planet too"

Whenever people are passionate about spreading the word for parrot conservation, it's a wonderful thing! Parrots are special birds, and they play important roles in their ecosystems. Unfortunately, people are too used to seeing them as pets and have forgotten how needed they are in the wild. That's why books like this are so important.

Note to the Reader

I am happy that you picked up this book and would like to share what inspired me to write it.

It all started during the depressing Covid period, when our freedom was snatched, and we were isolated from the outside world and confined to our homes.

What a dreadful time!

'This too shall pass,' that's how we consoled each other. Most of our time was spent in the balconies stretching out and trying to get some fresh air and during those times, I could see a parrot sitting in a beautiful white cage adjacent to my apartment. A small bell was tied to its feet. Now that I, too, was in the same shoes, I could so relate to its plight. There was a connection between us and I could empathize with its pain and suffering.

Gradually, we came out of the pandemic and moved toward normalcy. Sipping my hot cup of tea and inhaling the priceless freedom, my eyes caught the attention of my pandemic companion, i.e. my neighbour's pet parrot. And that's when a sudden throbbing pain hit my heart. Flashes of the scariest past came running to me and brought along some deeply nagging questions:

Do birds yearn for freedom just as we do?

Do they miss their loved ones like we do?

Do they crave companionship as we do?

And at that point in time, I realised that I would do my bit for these speechless creatures.

"I alone cannot change the world, but I can cast a stone across the waters to create many ripples." – Mother Teresa.

Sometimes, we feel that our efforts are small and insignificant, but a small ripple can gain momentum and create a storm that is insurmountable. If you feel concerned about your avian friends and want to contribute to helping them to lead a happy life, you must come forward and say NO to birds as pets.

And if you are holding this book in your hand, you have already taken your first step towards that cause.

Feel free to connect with me if you want to discuss more about the same. You can reach out to me at priya.hrdm@gmail.com

About The Author

Priya hails from the city of Prayagraj and is now settled in Mumbai along with her family. Priya has a passion for gardening. She is a nature lover and invests her leisure time with nature. Possessing an adventurous spirit, she loves traveling to new places, meeting new people, and engaging in new experiences.

With her cheerful personality and radiant positive vibes, she inspires her friends and family and motivates them to enjoy each and every moment of life.

Priya is among those who may not speak much, but her eyes will look out for details and positive observations. She has a very special, God-gifted skill of picking up things from life and enjoying them to the fullest.

Special Thanks

www.ingramcontent.com/pod-product-compliance
Lightning Source LLC
LaVergne TN
LVHW061617070526
838199LV00078B/7312